A *Baby Boomer's Times, Travels, Thoughts,* and *Hopes*

MARTIN FEESS

A BABY BOOMER'S TIMES, TRAVELS, THOUGHTS, AND HOPES

iUniverse books may be ordered through booksellers or by contacting:

iUniverse
1663 Liberty Drive
Bloomington, IN 47403
www.iuniverse.com
844-349-9409

ISBN: 978-1-5320-6275-9 (sc)
ISBN: 978-1-5320-6274-2 (e)

Library of Congress Control Number: 2018914462

Print information available on the last page.

iUniverse rev. date: 08/19/2020

Contents

For Karen, who has supported me in numerous endeavors over many years and shared many adventures.

Introduction

More babies were born in 1946 than ever before: 3.4 million, 20 percent more than in 1945. This was the beginning of the so-called "baby boom." In 1947, another 3.8 million babies were born; 3.9 million were born in 1952; and more than 4 million were born every year from 1954 until 1964, when the boom finally tapered off. By then, there were 76.4 million "baby boomers" in the United States. They made up almost 40 percent of the nation's population.[1]

The boom, of course, began because World War II ended in 1945 and young men and women who had long delayed forming families were eager to do so. The war, which had lasted four years for Americans, had been preceded by a decade of economic depression, during which the birthrate had been low. A new generation of parents embraced the new prosperity of the 1950s wholeheartedly. These parents, many of whom had very little when they were children, tended to indulge their own children. Baby boomers provided an economic boost as consumers. Manufacturers designed toys to serve a lucrative market—Barbie dolls, hula- hoops, yo-yos, toy guns, bicycles, sports equipment, etc. I had an arsenal of toy guns and a collection of baseball gloves and bats.

We, the American "baby boomers," are among the most privileged group of people to ever walk the earth. I have also had the unfair advantages of being white and male. I grew up in a stable (if slightly crazy) home environment in a small Wisconsin town, just big enough to have everything except serious crime. If I had not succeeded in life, there would have been no excuse for my failure.

---

[1] http://www.history.com/topics/baby-boomers

If I were not concerned with building a more just and more humane society, I would be selfish and irresponsible.

The boomers are a population bubble moving through American society. We have always been the largest group. As a result, we have always drawn the most attention from manufacturers, the film industry, the music industry, the food industry, the service industry, schools and universities, and, eventually, politicians. We are the spoiled generation, always demanding to get our way. Now that we are at retirement age, we are becoming a challenge (burden?) to our society. But it was not only the fortunate circumstances of birth which made us who we were. Like every other generation, we were affected by events. The Vietnam War is the signature event in the lives of baby boomers. It left a permanent impression and, for many, a permanent scar. Other influences which shaped my own views and personality include Walt Disney, the Cold War, Catholic elementary school, baseball, television, college in the early 1970s, the 9-11 tragedy, service in the Peace Corps, and episodes of residence abroad, which have included adventures in the Middle East, Eastern Europe, and Southeast Asia.

This is the story of a boomer's time as seen through a boomer's eyes. It is only about me in as much as my experiences in some ways typify the experiences of other boomers in similar situations or provide interesting or useful information and possible insight. I include my travels because they have informed my views, and because I want to encourage my fellow Americans to attempt to understand the perspectives of people in other places. Some of my experiences were humorous, and some provided me with life lessons which I have tried to impart in this account. As a historian, I believe that the greatest value of history is the lessons it provides for today and first person accounts are the most valuable. I have made my best effort to highlight the lesson of the last 70 years in this text. I also hope that the reader finds joy and cause for reflection in these reminiscences of a time before home computers and iPhones came to clutter and dominate our lives, as we look back in laughter, forward in hope, and attempt to better understand who we all are as Americans.

1

Dick and Jane, Walt Disney, and Television—The 1950s

In a conversation I once had with an elementary school teacher, I was shocked by her contention that the book which was used to teach me to read in first grade was a dirty book. Then I recalled some of the text and I saw that she was correct.

This was my introduction to literature. I never would have suspected any hidden, perverse meaning. I doubt that anyone else at that time did either. To my knowledge, no *Dick and Jane* scandal arose.

The 50s was an age of innocence and trust. I trusted all adults implicitly, reasoning that they knew about the world and I did not. I never would have even considered questioning my elementary teachers or any other adult placed in charge of me. Even when I was in high school, I naturally tended to give my teachers the benefit of the doubt. Kids are far different today.

Dick and Jane were trying to educate us. We can now jokingly speculate as to the scope of that intended education. At any rate, they were not alone in the endeavor. Walt Disney was making a serious effort to teach kids about American history. He taught us about Davy Crockett, the Sons of Liberty, and the Swamp Fox (Revolutionary War patriot Francis Marion).[2] Disney's version of history was wholesome, but artificially limited—all white. However, Walt did, in all fairness to him, reach out with an installment on Elfego Baca, whom Disney called "The Cat," but I still don't really know who this cat was. Walt Disney, as great as he was, was a man of his time. African-Americans and other minorities were invisible or ancillary in his stories, as they were in our American history books and American movies of that time. Indigenous people? Extinct? A significant portion of the population, which has played

---

[2] The starring role of Marion was played by a young Lesley Nielson, long before he made all those goofy comedies that some people secretly love.

a significant role all through American history, was absent. They were not included in the textbooks until they demanded inclusion. I don't believe that Hispanics have been accorded their fair place in Texas history either, even today.[3] These are things I think about now but never would have dreamt of in 1955, the year Disneyland opened. (I never would have dreamt that my grandmother's blue hair would become fashionable either.)

The civil rights movement saw some major milestones in the 50s, before mainstream America started to take much notice. In the 1954 Supreme Court case of *Brown vs. Board of Education* (of Topeka, Kansas), the Court issued a unanimous decision that "separate can never be equal," because by separating the races, society implies that one race is inferior, thus inflicting psychological damage which may be irreversible on members for the minority race. The Brown case nullified the previous (1896) decision of *Plessy vs. Ferguson,* which was that separate facilities did not violate the principle of "equal protection of the law" as long as they were equal. In practice, "separate" was strictly enforced in many places, but "equal" was never a serious consideration. Brown was the first of many landmark decisions made under Chief Justice Earl Warren.[4] A year after the Brown decision, Rosa Parks refused to give up her seat on a bus in Montgomery, Alabama. She was arrested and the young minister, Martin Luther King, Jr., organized a bus boycott. The boycott lasted a year and almost bankrupted the bus line. The Warren Court eventually weighed in on this too, striking down the bus segregation law.

President Eisenhower may not have been enthusiastic about the civil right movement, but he was serious about enforcing the law. In 1957 he sent 1,200 soldiers of the US Army to Little Rock,

---

[3] PBS did an excellent, though slightly romanticized, dramatic presentation of the life of San Antonio major and fighter for Texas independence, Juan Seguin, *Seguin*, which I would recommend to anyone who is interested in the Chicano story of the Texas war for independence.

[4] President Eisenhower had appointed Warren in 1953. Many people consider Warren to have been one of the greatest Chief Justices of all times, but Eisenhower disagreed. He came to regret the appointment.

Thurgood Marshall was the attorney for Brown. He later became the first African-American appointed as a Justice of the Supreme Court and served for many years with distinction.

Arkansas and placed the state National Guard under his authority to protect nine African-American students who insisted on their right to enroll at Little Rock Central High School against the wishes of Arkansas Governor Orville Faubus. This was the first time since Reconstruction that federal troops had been sent into the South to protect African-Americans, and many stayed in Little Rock until the end of November to continue to protect those students, who endured harassment all year. Central High School was closed the following year, and the African-American students had to go elsewhere.[5] Segregation in the old South would not be easily defeated regardless of any Supreme Court ruling.

Television in the 1950s

I am just young enough that I do not remember a time when we did not have television. Large, gaudy antennas were mounted on every house. TV stations broadcasted from about 6AM until about midnight, signing off with the national anthem or "God Bless America". *TV Guide* was the most widely circulated magazine in America when I was a young child. *The Lone Ranger* was still a radio series, but it was also on television, one of the popular westerns which dominated the new medium in the 1950s. Most of these westerns were morality plays with lessons about courage, justice, and self-sacrifice directed at children, with enough action to entertain the entire family. The best of the westerns were, however, aimed at the adult audience. Popular adult westerns in the 50s were *Rawhide, Wagon Train, Maverick*, and *Gunsmoke*. The first three of these were an hour long, as opposed to the standard half hour venue. This allowed the writers enough time to tell a more nuanced story with more interesting characters than the cardboard stereotypes of the half hour show. Brett Maverick (James Garner) was a professional gambler who never cheated, but could expose any cheater. He also often professed "I'm a coward" which viewers came to realize meant "I'm a regular guy and I do not want to be a hero." But, of course, he was capable of being a hero when pushed into the role, which is as we want to see ourselves. He would always, in the end, do the right thing. *Maverick,* which is sometimes

---

[5] Bates, Daisy, "Integration of Central High School: Little Rock Nine," *History Channel,* http://www.history.com/topics/black-history/central-high-school-integration.

described are a comedy-western, may have been the most popular TV western of that time both for children and adults. It provided a refreshing change for the formula half hour westerns.

In the stereotypical westerns of the time, the "good guys" would always do the right thing and no one, not even the villains, cussed. The easy way to provide western screen heroes was for them to be "lawmen." One of the many of these westerns was actually entitled *Lawman*. The prototype for the TV western "lawman" was *Wyatt Earp*, played by Hugh O'Brien, and this show was probably the best of the lot. But you could only have so many lawmen. Josh Randall (Steve McQueen) was a bounty hunter in *Wanted Dead or Alive*. Not surprisingly, he always brought his man in alive, an unlikely scenario in reality. The dashing Paladin (Richard Boone) was a "hired gun" in *Have Gun, Will Travel*. He apparently had such a good business that he could afford to be selective about his clients. He never took the role of a hired thug but fought against many. Other television western heroes included a Wells Fargo investigator (*Tales of Wells Fargo*), a "sod buster" (farmer in *The Rifleman*), an Apache chief (*Broken Arrow*), a cowgirl (*Annie* Oakley), a law student by correspondence (*Sugar Foot*), and a cavalry dog (Corporal *Rin Tin Tin*). *Death Valley Days* purported to tell true stories of the old west, hosted by "the Old Ranger" until he got too old and was replaced by the B movie actor, Ronald Reagan. There were two notable exceptions to the Anglo hero in the westerns. The Cisco Kid was a Hispanic-American western hero played by a Hispanic actor. This series was as popular as most other Saturday morning westerns for children, but prime time spots, which the whole family might watch, seemed to have been for Anglos only until the special Disney magic brought Zorro, a character from dime novels, to the television screen. This series was popular in prime time due to Disney's genius at storytelling with lots of playful humor. Unfortunately, this incarnation of Zorro was portrayed by an Italian-American, and he fought the corrupt government of Spanish California, protecting the hapless Hispanic population there.

Of course these small screen efforts were a launching stage to many movie careers and a stopping off point for some already well-known actors. Burt Reynolds had begun his career as a stunt man for the movies before landing a recurring acting role on *Gunsmoke* as the town blacksmith. Clint Eastwood was a regular as Rowdy Yates on *Rawhide*. Nick Adams had the lead role as Johnny Yuma, *The Rebel*, and Johnny Cash sang the theme song, *The Rebel*

(Johnny Yuma). Steve McQueen, as has been mentioned, had the lead role in *Wanted Dead or Alive.* Richard Boone became a star when he brought his rich talents to the Paladin character in *Have Gun-Will Travel.* Chuck Connors had been a professional baseball player trying to break in to the big leagues when he became *The Rifleman.* This led him to a variety of roles, mainly in television, and a long acting career. And *Maverick* made the young James Garner popular and sought after by movie makers. John Wayne was still cranking out epic westerns for the big screen, but he was middle age by the 1950. Roy Rogers was more popular with my generation. He was the star of many western movies and his own Saturday morning television series.

I don't believe that all those hours of television westerns I watched as a young child were entirely wasted. The heroes of these westerns modeled a strict moral code. This guided me, and I'm sure, many others in our early years. I know that this is corny. The world of TV westerns was black and white, sanitized, and idealized, unlike the dirty, colorful real world which is fraught with compromise. But young children need to be insulated by a sanitized, idealized world. When one negotiates the real world and makes compromises, a moral compass is essential for a meaningful life. The westerns encouraged the development of such a moral compass. I also got lots of examples of correct English from the westerns. The heroes and many of the villains always spoke correct English. I learned correct, proper English from TV westerns, not from home. I also learned not to cuss from television and from home. Bad language was nonexistent to me in my earliest years. As an adult, I have rarely felt the need to add profanity to my speech. I see no value in it. Taken literally, most profane expressions actually sound stupid if you think about it. In the 50s, we didn't have *Sesame Street* and didn't need it; we had *Gunsmoke.*

Television was experimental in the 50s. Live dramas were attempted at first and failed. Serious television dramas were rare in the 50s. The country had little taste for them after the serious, real life and deadly dramas of World War II and the Great Depression. However, audiences found some fascination with the macabre. *Twilight Zone* with Rod Serling and *Alfred Hitchcock Presents* were both high quality. Television's national news was only on for 15 minutes. Situation comedies were not as numerous as westerns, but there were some very popular early sitcoms. *I Love Lucy* with Lucille Ball and Desi Arnaz and *The Honeymooners* staring Jackie

Gleason topped the list. Jackie played Ralph Kramden, a Brooklyn bus driver whose wife, Alice, always antagonized him by pointing out his errors of judgment, and he would responded by threatening to hit her so hard he would send her "to the moon, Alice, to the moon". But he never hurt her in any way, and they usually ended up hugging at the end with Gleason telling her "Baby, you're the greatest."[6]

Leave It to Beaver started a little later than these and endured way too long. "The Beaver," Jerry Mathers, was cute talking like a second grader when he was about 7. But by the time the series ended Jerry Mathers was about 14 and the writers still had him saying the same types of lines, so he sounded foolish. Beaver's father, Ward Cleaver, played by Hugh Beaumont, was the typical television father of that time--kind, concerned, wise, and thoughtful. He was also open-minded and willing to take advice from his wife, the perfect stay at home mom, June. Barbara Billingsley played June Cleaver and delivered some lines which are awkward today and somewhat humorous when taken out of context.

The most likeable sitcom couples of that time were real married couples like Lucy and Desi. We watched George Burns and Gracie Allen in *The Burns and Allen Show,* and *Ozzie and Harriett,* the Nelson's. The Nelson's used their show to help propel their son, Ricky Nelson, to rock-and–roll stardom. George Burns seemed content to play straight-man to Gracie's wildly distorted logic, while telling an occasional joke himself. Gracie had a sweet, irresistible charm, and George had an easy-going manner (always with a cigar in his hand) which ingratiated him to audiences. He ended up living to the age of 99, outliving her by decades, and he always spoke with reverence and affection about her. TV families were so nice that those of us living in working class, lower middle class, or marginal class families, where people frequently screamed and yelled, might think *What is wrong with us?* That thought certainly occurred to me.

At least two variety shows garnered large audiences in the 50s. *The Gary Moore Show* showcased the talents of young Carol Burnett, and the *Ed Sullivan Show* had whole families watching together as Ed attempted to have some portion of each show directed to each specific age group. The most well remembered portion of the *Sullivan Show* was the musical guest segment for the teenage

---

[6] Alice was played by Audrey Meadows and Ralph's neighbor and best friend, Ed Norton, was played by Art Carney.

audience. The performers were the latest new, popular singers and groups making their television debuts. We saw Elvis Presley as he was starting off. The Beatles performed on *The Sullivan Show*, singing "I Wanna Hold Your Hand" during their first tour of the US in early 1964. That same year Michael Jackson appeared on the show as the child star of The Jackson Five. The hot, new Rolling Stones wanted to sing their song "Let's Spend the Night Together" on *The Sullivan Show*, but they changed the lyrics to "Let's spend some time together" at Sullivan's insistence. *The Ed Sullivan Show* was such an important springboard for new musical talent that most would bow to Ed's strict standards. Two of the popular comedians of the time, Jack Benny and Red Skeleton, also had comedy-variety shows which attracted large numbers of viewers, though Benny was "only 39," a claim that was always good for a laugh along with Benny's violin serenades. Less well remembered today is *The Jimmy Durante Show*, which Durante signed-off every week with "Goodnight Mrs. Calabash wherever you are."

"Housewives" of the day were watching soap operas. *As the World Turns* was the popular early "soap" which ran for decades. And yes, the term "soap opera" is derived from the fact that the sponsors were often detergent manufacturers advertising to stay-at-home moms who were still commonly referred to as "housewives." In the early 50s, this group constituted half of the married women in America. Willingly or not, "Rosie the Riveter" and many her cohorts had retired from working outside the home to make room for returning veterans after the war. Those women who chose to stay in the work force could expect to make about half the wage of a man, even for the same job. This wage discrimination was open, and the justification that the man would have a family to support was seriously accepted as the way of the world. Television reflected this condition. June Cleaver, Lucy Ricardo, Alice Kramden, and Harriet Nelson were all "housewives," and much of the humor in *I Love Lucy* was built around the fact that Lucy had dreams, goals, and ambitions of her own. (Ozzie Nelson didn't seem to have a job either.)

African-Americans were nearly completely absent from American television in the 1950s. I can only really think of two exceptions. Jack Benny had a black servant names Rochester. And, surprisingly, one show had an all-black cast every week. That was *Amos and Andy*. The show had been popular on the radio. The two main characters were George Stephens, "the Kingfish", who was a manipulative schemer, and Andy, a rather dull witted fellow who was often deceived by the Kingfish. The depiction of African-Americans with these crude stereotypes was disgraceful. But what I found interesting about the show was that all the people in it were black, including police officers, judges, business leaders, etc. Amos, who was not actually a main character, was a wise cab driver who often counselled his friend, Andy. In the world I saw on a daily basis, there were no black police officers, or black judges, or black business leaders. *Amos and Andy* was a terrible show in that it perpetuated black stereotypes with Andy and the Kingfish, and even to a lesser extent with Amos. But in its time, it was the only place in America I saw the possibility of African-American judges. That's how racially backward white America was in a time not that long ago.

2

Society in the 1950s

The 1950s were truly the old world. The telephones we had were attached to the wall via a line, and they had no dial. When you picked up the phone you would hear the operator say, "Number please?" Milk was delivered to peoples' houses in reusable bottles. Elevators employed operators. We got our gas at service stations, at which an attendant pumped the gas, washed the windshield, and checked the oil. Some service stations also gave you a free glass with a minimum purchase. Passenger trains still ran in most cities. Computers were huge monstrosities which took up large rooms and could only be found in large government organizations or very large universities. And all our music was on vinyl or the AM radio. The juke box played six songs for a quarter.

I liked Ike. Everybody did. Dwight D. Eisenhower, the hero of World War II, was the president from 1953 through January 1961. I was three when President Truman left office. I have no memory of him being president, but I remember Ike well. Democratic Party critics were saying that we should elect Ben Hogan as president, because if we are going to have a golfer in the White House, he might just as well be a good one. Ike played a lot of golf as president. Looking back on his presidency, he really didn't take the lead with many major initiatives and much of the country seemed okay with that. Though African-Americans were clamoring for change, most white Americans seemed to desire calm and stability more than anything. This was the time when white Americans were enjoying a good life, which they felt was well-earned by service in World War II. As president, former General Eisenhower appointed competent people, set them to doing their jobs, and hit the golf course.

He allowed the Congress to take a lead role, and Congress appeared to function well, often in a somewhat bipartisan manner which should be a model for Congress today. The Warren (Supreme) Court was slowly advancing the cause of civil rights, at times to the chagrin of the President, but with his support. Eisenhower's legacy,

9

however, is hallmarked by the big, beautiful interstate highway system constructed under the *Federal-Aid Highways Act of 1956.*

Before this time, Route 66 had become famous as "the mother road," the main road from Chicago to Los Angeles. A famous song was written about Route 66, and a popular television series depicted the adventures of two travelers on the road. This two lane highway wound through towns all along the way. Many towns had Route 66 as their Main Street, and the traffic on the road was essential to the success of businesses in these towns. The new super highway system changed America, killing a way of life for some, but opening opportunities for the majority. The 1950s were, more than anything, years of increasing opportunity.

The most transformative trend, outside of the emerging civil rights movement, was the rapid democratization of higher education which had begun because of the 1944 *GI Bill.* Suddenly scores of young men, who would never have thought higher education to be possible for them, were entering colleges and universities all over the US in the immediate post-war years. These new college students were mature, battle hardened, focused, and determined to make the most of this surprising opportunity. These newly educated men provided a boom in brain power, which propelled unprecedented economic expansion. Then colleges and universities, which had expanded to accommodate the veterans, had the problem of continuing to recruit talented students or face the need for sudden, painful contraction. Thus the boomers may have been the greatest beneficiaries of the *GI Bill,* as universities strove to accommodate us by keeping costs down.

After having been propelled forward by the *GI Bill*, American higher education received another boost from the perceived threat of the Cold War. The Soviets were first to launch a satellite into space (Sputnik) in 1957. At President Eisenhower's direction, Congress leaped into action with the *National Defense Education Act of 1958,* and Eisenhower established NASA (National Aeronautics and Space Administration). The *National Defense Education Act* provided financial aid for students of science and math and other funding for university science programs. Both the NDEA and the creation of NASA had far reaching results which put the US on track to lead the world in both education and space exploration. And the university doors were flung wide open for the boomers.

I am saddened to see the doors of higher education closing on young people today. Expectations have been permanently raised, but access is no longer painless. I was able to go through college self-funding with the help of the GI Bill and emerge debt free. I later attended graduate school, obtaining an MA debt free, and followed that some years later with a debt free Ph.D. Today, students emerge from college with $30,000 or more of debt. This is a stressful burden on these graduates and a drag on our economy. As a high school teacher, I have tried to encourage students to attend community college for the first two years, thus greatly reducing the cost of their education. The societal problem which needs to be addressed here is *How can colleges bring costs down enough to make tuitions affordable again?* Are university professors overpaid? Universities (and professors) argue that competition from the private sector pushes salaries up. My state, Arizona, was considering enhancing opportunities by upgrading several large community colleges to four year undergraduate institution (without research programs), but the recession of 2008 hit and the proposal seems to have been scrapped. University cost, like any other serious problem, is complex, but can be solved with serious discussed among people sincerely committed to solving the problem.

Eisenhower, as the Republican presidential nominee, was opposed twice by Adlai Stevenson, the Democratic choice in both 1952 and 1956. Stevenson, the intellectual governor of Illinois, may well have been the best man ever to have run for president twice without being elected. A story is told of him that after one of his speeches an enthusiastic member of the audience said to him, "Governor Stevenson, all thinking people are for you!" to which Stevenson replied, "That's not enough. I need a majority."[7]
Eisenhower and Stevenson were both good men, who could put the good of the country ahead of party or politics. Had Stevenson been elected, though, the civil rights movement would have found an advocate in the White House, and we might not have had the close collaboration between the State Department and the CIA which evolved under Ike. Ike's Secretary of State was John Foster Dulles and his CIA director was brother, Allan Dulles. Under Allan Dulles the CIA developed programs of "covert operations," manipulation to control the politics of other countries.
However disturbing the marriage of the State Department and the CIA were under Eisenhower, he was not naive about the

---

[7] "Music Cues: Adlai Stevenson. February 5, 2000," NPR https://www.npr.org/programs/wesat/000205.stevenson.html

military. This five star general was wise enough to see that the military would always continue to demand bigger, better, and more weapons and equipment, and more manpower than was prudent, while industrialists would push to be allowed to supply the military with all it demanded, thus diverting scarce resources away from the creation of consumer goods. Sure, we could have full employment this way, but consumer goods would be more limited and more expensive, and everyone would be poorer as a result. Eisenhower resisted these pressures, pinched nickels, and produced a balance or nearly balanced budget every year of his tenure. After eight years of budget battles, Ike gave a farewell address in January 1961 warning the nation of the danger that the "military-industrial complex" would demand so much that the society would come to serve the military, rather than the other way around.[8]

Ike's Farewell Address didn't make for big news then, because times were good in the 50s. Even the constant threat of nuclear holocaust didn't deter Americans from having a good time. I and my cohorts never did the "duck and cover" drill in preparation for a nuclear attack, as did children who were a little older. I think that the reality had set-in regarding survival possibilities by the time we entered school in the mid-1950s, and the government knew that all anyone could really do in such a case was to put one's head between his knees and kiss his butt goodbye. The threat was still considered to be real though. When John Kennedy became president in 1961, he encouraged Americans to build bomb shelters, and many people all over the country took him seriously, constructing hundreds of thousands of such doomsday burrows.

Sure I liked Ike, but I loved Marilyn Monroe. Marilyn had a wonderful warm charm, and she had a natural brilliance as a comedy actress. No one since can compare. She was sexy, smart, beaming with life, and she always appeared to be genuine. I was even seduced by her singing. *Gentlemen Prefer Blonds* is still a joy to watch even after all the times I've seen it. *Some Like it Hot* and *The Seven Year Itch* are her other two most famous comedies. In both she lights up the screen and outperforms some of the best known

---

[8] The speech was, in part, an answer to President-elect Kennedy's assertion of a "missile gap" during the 1960 campaign. Eisenhower's speech was a wise warning, which has always been relevant and is more relevant today than it has been for a long time. In that speech, Eisenhower coined the term "military-industrial complex."

actors of the time: Jack Lemmon, Tony Curtis, Joe E. Brown, and Tom Ewell. In *The Prince and the Showgirl,* she steals the show from the great Sir Lawrence Olivier, and her persona saves this otherwise lackluster film. Monroe could also show endearing vulnerability, as she did in the drama *River of No Return* (in addition to singing the title song). I don't mean to say that Marilyn was a saint. Her dark side included a thinly veiled affair she had with President John Kennedy. But I didn't care. Marilyn's real name was Norma Jean. Elton John stated well what many others felt with his touching tribute song, "Candle in the Wind"

Goodbye Norma Jean
Though I never knew you
You had the grace to hold yourself
While those around you crawled
They crawled out of the woodwork
And they whispered into your brain
They set you on the treadmill
And they made you change your name.[9]

And I too would have liked to love her "but I was just a kid. The candle burned out long ago but the legend never did."[10] Marilyn died tragically from an overdose of sleeping pills in 1963 at the age of 36.

I was never a big Elvis Presley fan, but he also had a special gift and a special presence like Marilyn. His life story and tragic death beg comparison with Marilyn. Elvis had a unique singing voice which may have been better suited to powerful ballads than to rock and roll. Most people know that Elvis had countless gold and platinum records. But what most people do not know is that Elvis won only two Grammies and both were in the category "Gospel Music." Like Marilyn, Elvis had an affable demeanor. Despite all his success, he appeared genuinely modest. His downfall occurred because he trusted too much. He allowed others to make decisions for him. He wanted to be an actor and showed some promise in his first movie, *Charro.* Of all the Elvis Presley movies, this is the only one in which he does not sing, though he did sing the title song for the credits. After that he played some semi-serious roles in the

---

[9] John, Elton, "Candle in the Wind," *Goodbye Yellow Brick Road,* Gus Dudgeon producer, MCA, 1973. Elton John would adapt this song years later to honor Princess Diana after her tragic death.
[10] Ibid.

beginning. *Love Me Tender* and *Kid Galahad* were both of this type. But the movie makers had to feature him singing in both, and they saw a sure money maker. He came to star in numerous musicals which were forgettable at best and often plain silly. He started to find himself as a live performer in Las Vegas, but he had slipped into drug use (prescription) and he had a quack doctor who was willing to write these prescriptions. He died in 1977 at the age of 42.

Rock-and-roll music did not start with Elvis. It evolved from African-American music. Elvis may have been "the king of rock-and-roll", but the real father of rock-and-roll was an African-American, Chuck Berry. Though Elvis's story is tragic, he had the opportunity to chart his own way, if he had so chosen. The door was open to him. Chuck Berry had a more difficult road to acceptance. Berry's music was on par with that of Elvis, arguably better. Despite some reluctance by mainstream radio stations to play his music, Berry would have eleven top ten hits between 1955 and 1961.[11] He was an original and may have been too far ahead of his time, but the fact that he was black in the 50s was probably a limiting factor for his career. I love Chuck Berry music, but I don't remember being much aware of him as I was growing up. I never heard him on the radio, but maybe this is because he was before my time. I did see Berry as the featured performer in a rock-and-roll revival concert in the 1978, and I saw him again in the 1990s on tour in some small venue. Both were a thrill for me, but the fact that the great Chuck Berry was still struggling enough in his later years to need to perform in an ensemble on the road in the 70s and still on the road in the 90s is unsettling.[12]

Throughout the 1950s and 1960s the "big three" Detroit automobile makers, GM, Ford, and Chrysler led the world in car sales with big, beautiful, and highly dependable automobiles, the best in the world. A fourth automaker, American Motors (AMC) was also producing excellent quality autos. AMC may have been too far ahead of its time though. The AMC Ramblers were fuel efficient which meant that they were not as fast or powerful as the GM cars. They were also ugly. My family owned an ugly AMC Nash

---

[11] Cowan, Tom and Jack Maguire, *Timelines of African-American History*, (Roundtable Press, Inc., 1994), p. 226.

[12] "Maybellene" is my favorite Chuck Berry song. I would advise anyone not already familiar with Chuck Berry music to do yourself a favor and listen.

which vaguely resembled a tank. Its greatest redeeming quality to me was that it had a standard transmission, so I learned to drive a standard transmission vehicle from the beginning. The Nash was a far cry from my dream car though. I would rather have been driving the new Mustang, which Ford had introduced to the market in 1962. Ralph Nader might have greatly disagreed with my praise of American autos. In 1965, the year of the classic Mustang, he published *Unsafe at Any Speed*, which accused the American auto makers of callous disregard for safety. Mandatory seatbelt laws were one result of Nader's book.

Saturday matinee movies were a big part of my childhood. Admission was 20 cents for kids under 12. There were usually two or three cartoons prior to the feature presentation and sometimes there was a double feature. In 1964 the second James Bond film, *From Russia with Love*, came out. It played in my town as a double feature with the first James Bond, *Doctor No,* which I had not yet seen. Wow! I was an instant fan and have been ever since. We had two movie theaters in my town—no multiplex. There was no such thing. Our theaters were big and beautiful--both on Main Street, not in a mall. There was no such thing as a mall either. But the downtown was vibrant. This is where everyone went to shop. Our Main Street featured Woolworth's, Kresge's, J.J. Newberry, and Sears, among other stores, our two large movie theaters, some restaurants and bars, and a bowling alley. I never saw a Walmart until the late 1980s. That downtown area of my hometown is almost all gone now, replaced by banks and office buildings. It was killed by a mall. The mall that killed it isn't doing too well now either.

A new fast food burger restaurant called McDonalds opened in my town around 1958 boasting "over one billion sold" and advertising a full meal and "change back for your dollar." True, I would get two hamburgers, an order of fries, and a chocolate shake for 85 cents. Everything was cheap in the 1950s. A bottomless cup of coffee was ten cents in any restaurant. A twelve ounce coke was 8 cents plus a 2 cent deposit on the bottle. The government wanted children to drink milk, so a government subsidized program provided two half pint size containers of milk for 2 cents every day with school lunch. The teachers collected a dime from every student once a week to pay for milk for that week.

We also contributed dimes to the "March of Dimes", a charity formed to support research to eradicate polio. Jonas Salk and Albert

Sabin both actually developed their polio vaccines with the help of funds granted by the March of Dimes. I never made the connection to the late president and polio sufferer, Franklin Roosevelt on the dime then, but he actually founded the program in 1938. Because of the success of its original goal, the March of Dimes still exists today, supporting other medical research to combat complications of birth. Polio was the scourge of the 50s and early 60s. Before the polio vaccines were developed, 15,000 Americans per year suffered paralysis due to the disease.[13] I had a close friend who had suffered from it and recovered, but always walked with a limp.

Though I never contracted polio, I got everything else—measles, mumps, chickenpox. I also got frequent colds, probably because I did not wash my hands enough. I was not taught much about hygiene. I missed a lot of school in the early grades. Add to that the fact that I was an apathetic student, and you get the picture of a boy far behind with few prospects for catching up. My school did not have special education. Thank God! I would certainly have been in it. I already had a poor self-image. I remember that I tried to keep a healthy perspective on it, thinking, *Some people have to be stupid. I guess I'm one of those.* Placement in special education would have further affirmed my self-assessment. I failed second grade too. My plight was compounded by the fact that I was big for my age. I was the biggest kid in my class **before** I failed. My second year in second grade was deeply humiliating. My point here is that while special education and being "held back" may be good for some students, they are not good for everyone. Being held back almost ruined my life. Special education would have been even more demoralizing.

Those students who are "held back" should somehow be allowed a possibility for catching up and those students placed in special education should be encourage to work their way out. Some opportunities for catching up, such as summer programs and online classes, do exist today. I was provided with a solution which worked for me and was more cost effective. I was allowed to skip third grade and prove myself in fourth grade (without special education). I know that special education is supposed to be directing students to work their way out, but as a teacher in the public schools, I have seen in practice that students admitted into special education tend to stay in special education until they finish high school. Special education

---

[13] "Polio Elimination in the United States," Center of Disease Control and Elimination, last updated in 2017, https://www.cdc.gov/polio/us

becomes a comfortable place to underachieve. This is a trap into which I could easily have fallen. On the other hand, being allowed to skip third grade was one of the best things that ever happened to me, and I was now determined to never fail in school again.

Catholic School

I had started my academic career in public school with Dick and Jane but transferred to Catholic school for grades four through eight. After my two years in second grade, I had found salvation and my chance for redemption. Catholic school was great for language arts, social studies, and math. However, music, art, and science were all but nonexistent. The only exception was the church children's choir for which I had no talent. Literacy was the top priority in Catholics schools. We didn't just have English; we studied language (grammar), spelling, and reading—three distinct subjects. Social studies was all about history and geography. We had history and geography every year from fifth grade on. I never took spelling seriously which is part of why I have always been a bad speller, but I excelled in grammar. We diagrammed sentences nearly every day, and I found that I actually enjoyed diagramming sentences and learned from the process. This has always helped my writing and has made me a competent writing teacher.

Geography every year helped provide me with a broader understanding and fascination with the world, but nothing excited me like history. The history lessons in Catholic school ignited a passion in mc that still burns today. These were inspiring stories of great men and great women (mostly great men as it was taught then). I wanted to ride with Charlemagne and serve under Grant. I wanted to ride the hobo trains of the 1930s. I wanted to storm the beach on D-Day. And today, I would like talk with Plato about that cave and get his ideas about an escape plan for mankind. I am indebted to my Catholic school education for what it has made me, but for those students with inclination toward science, art, or music, my Catholic school would have been an impoverishing environment.

When I returned to the public system for grades nine through twelve, there was nothing particularly inspiring about it. The math education provided in Catholic schools then was somewhat limited, but excellent in what it did cover. We never touched algebra or proportions, but I knew fractions, decimals, and percents inside and out, and I could solve any word problem that did not absolutely require algebra. I remember frustrating my ninth grade algebra teacher by solving nearly every word problem without algebra. I felt completely competent and comfortable with math.

The other thing that was distinctive and valuable about Catholic school is the strong focus on character development, self-discipline, and the sacred. Do your best; be your best; and think about how your actions affect others. I learned that all people are equal, because everyone's life is sacred and needs to be respected at all times. And I learned that somethings like honor, loyalty and courage, are sacred. As a history teacher, I have always treated Armistice Day, November 11, as a sacred day. November 11, 1918 was the day that World War I ended. According to the American president, Woodrow Wilson, this had been the "war to end all wars." Armistice Day celebrated this vision as more than just a hope. Later when ending all wars appeared to have been a fantasy, Armistice Day became Veterans Day in America. I prefer the name "Armistice Day" because it is an assertion of a sacred goal worth striving for. The fact that this is one of the few remaining national holidays not moved to Mondays is a nod to the sanctity of the day, November 11.

Self-discipline and individual responsibility are also important to me. My self-disciple, and that of my classmates, was a practical necessity for my class to function. My class (grade level) was the smallest in the school. So we were always in a double grade with the next grade below us. We had about 22 students in my grade and the grade below us had about 22 students of their grade in the same room and taught by the same teacher. So the poor teacher had more than 40 students in two grades in the same room. She (or one year it was he) taught the one grade while the other grade worked quietly. All the students had to have the self-discipline to work in perfect (or near perfect) silence for half of the school day; and we did. The nuns taught this way year after year, but I don't remember a lay teacher who ever came back after the first year.

All my teachers in the Catholic school were totally dedicated and kind. It was a wonderfully, nurturing environment. I would later learn that some, maybe most, public school teachers were just as wonderful, but not all. One ninth grade teacher I remember always seemed angry and belligerent to us, and he would frequently make an obscene gesture at us, pretending to be pushing up his glasses.

Much of the religious training in Catholic school was really about issues of right and wrong in our interactions with others. I have heard Protestants joke about "Catholic guilt." I don't think that guilt is necessarily bad. When you do something wrong, you should feel guilty. Guilt is just a component of a healthy moral compass. However, guilt by itself is not healthy. Healthy guilt requires action to make amends and a resolve to not reoffend. I never felt that confession gave me license to reoffend.

The religious training we received in Catholic school was not brainwashing exactly. It was well intentioned. If we were to call ourselves Catholic, we should know the teachings of the faith. We attended mass every day, so we heard a daily lesson from the Old Testament (an angry God), the New Testament (Jesus stories), and the Epistles (letter of St. Paul). Our religion classes, however, did not follow up on the lessons learned that day at mass or focus on the Bible. The focus was on the catechism. We memorized hundreds of questions and answers verbatim in case some wise ass Protestant would ever ask. I was never asked. I have kept the good values I gained through my Catholic education and long ago discarded the dogma. I'm a reformed Catholic. I don't attend church services, but the Catholic Church is the one I don't attend.

Major Cultural and World Events of the 1950s

1952	*Diary of Anne Frank* is published.[14]	Anne Frank kept the diary as a teenage girl for two years in which her family hid from the Nazis in an attic during World War II. Unfortunately the family was discovered and Miss Frank did not survive the war.
1953	Tenzing Norgay and Edmund Hillary are the first humans to climb to the top of Mount Everest.	This was Sherpa guide Norgay's seventh attempt and Hillary's second.
1953	Joseph Stalin dies.	Stalin had subverted the Soviet state into what was called a "cult of personality" and a "great terror," and was responsible for more executions than Adolf Hitler.
1954	Roger Bannister breaks the four minute mile.	Bannister's official time was 3:59.4. He was the first man to run the mile in under 4 minutes.[15]
1955	Disneyland opens.	I never gave a thought to going there. California was like the other side of the world.

---

[14] Kate Phelps and Fiona Courtenay-Thompson, managing editors, The Twentieth Century Year by Year (London: Marshall Publishing, 1998) p. 187.

[15] Ibid. p. 196.

1956	Boxer Rocky Marciano retires undefeated.	Rocky weighed only about 185 pounds, but he was the world heavy weight champion with 49 wins and no loses. He had won 43 of his bouts by knockout.[16]
1956	Don Larson pitches the first World Series perfect game.	Yankee Don Larson faced only 27 Brooklyn Dodger batters and retired them all.[17]
1957	Jack Kerouac publishes *On the Road.*[18]	*On the Road* became the unofficial bible of "the beat generation."
1959	Alaska becomes the 49th state.	

---

[16] Ibid. p. 203.
[17] Ibid, p. 205.
[18] Ibid. p. 207.

3

The Swinging 60s

Baseball—Swinging a Bat

Baseball really isn't the national pastime anymore, but it was in the 1960s. Televised games, however, were rare then. Only a few select games, usually the Yankees, were televised on Saturdays and Sundays. I followed the Milwaukee Braves everyday on the radio.[19] I was an avid fan so I also followed all the other teams as much as possible. The Yankees always drew everyone's attention. In those days players signed what amounted to a lifetime contract (or sentence) to play for one team. Because the Yankees had deep pockets, they were able to go all over the country signing the best players. So, the Yankees had as much talent on their farm teams (minor league affiliates) as many other major league teams had on the regular roster.

In the summer of 1961 Mickey Mantle and Roger Maris were thrilling baseball fans everywhere by hitting home runs. By the middle of that summer the big sporting news was that Mantle or Maris or both might break Babe Ruth's long-standing single season home run record (60 home runs). As I listened to my Braves games on the radio, the announcers were listening for word of another Yankee home run, and would report it instantly. Ruth had set the record in 1927 when the season was only 154 games long. In the longer 162 games season of modern times, Roger Maris had 59 home runs at the 154 game mark. He hit two more after that. His 61st home run was hit in the last game of the season. Mickey Mantle was admitted to the Baseball Hall of Fame long ago. I should also mention that Mantle had a reputation as a near perfect all-around player. He maintained a high batting average and was considered to have been an excellent center fielder. He was

---

[19] The Braves moved to Milwaukee from Boston in 1953 and remained in Milwaukee until the mid-1960s, when they moved to Atlanta.

selected to the American League All-Star team 20 times. And he hit several towering, legendary home runs which were estimated to have traveled well in excess of 500 feet. Roger Maris has not yet been selected to the Hall of Fame, but the bat with which he hit that 61st home run is there.

Of course the Yankees had other players who also excited fans. Whitey Ford was their ace pitcher. He compiled a record of 25 wins and 4 losses that year. Ford was a unique artist on the mound. He consistently had a low ERA (earning run average), but fewer strikeouts than you might expect. He said that he would rather get an out with one pitch than have to throw three pitches for it. He pitched for 16 seasons with the Yankees and compiled a winning rate of .690. He is also in the Hall of Fame, as is his catcher, the great Yogi Berra. (By the way, Yogi Bear is named after him, not the other way around). Yogi was a great catcher, a great hitter, a home run hitter, and a somewhat renowned philosopher. He actually published several books which are collections of the oddly confused and enlightened sayings which have come to be known as "Yogiisms". Among the best known of these are: "It ain't over till it's over," "You have to go to other people's funerals, or they won't come to yours," "Baseball is 90% mental; the other half is physical," "When you arrive at a fork in the road, take it," and "If you don't know where you are going, you might wind up some place else." Mantle, Maris, Ford, and Berra are my four favorite Yankees because they were all great players and genuinely modest. They did not need to tell anyone how great they were. They just played the game—people knew.

The 1950s and 60s, which these Yankees dominated, were the Golden Age of Baseball. National League players of that time, who are icons today, were the Dodger pitchers Sandy Koufax and Don Drysdale, Henry "Hammerin' Hank" Aaron and Warren Spahn of my Milwaukee Braves, Ernie "Mr. Cub" Banks, Stan "The Man" Musial of the Cardinals, and Willie "Say Hey" Mays, the giant of the Giants. Sandy Koufax simply overwhelmed hitters in the 60s. He won the Cy Young Award as the best pitcher in baseball three times—1963, 65, and 66--and was also chosen as the National League MVP (Most Valuable Player) in 1963, a remarkable, and very rare, honor for a starting pitcher, who only plays every fourth day. Left-hander Koufax, who was known for the overpowering speed of his fastball, had struggled with control problems in his early years and almost gave up on baseball. According to Koufax himself, success came when he realized that he did not need to throw as hard as he could to get batters out. After "slowing down" his fastball, Koufax often led the league in strikeouts and earned run average (ERA). His meteoric career ended suddenly after his 1966 Cy Young year because he developed arthritis in his left elbow.

Only Koufax could have overshadowed Don Drysdale, his teammate, who had to settle for being the second best Dodger pitcher in the 60s, though he could claim to be the best right handed pitcher in baseball. Drysdale, a side-arm fast-baller, won the Cy Young Award in 1962. But he is best remembered for pitching six straight shutouts and a total of 58 2/3 consecutive shutout innings in 1968. If his career had not paralleled that of Koufax, he would probably be considered the premier pitcher in 1960s baseball, though Bob Gibson of the Cardinals would also have some claim to that title.

Henry Aaron broke Babe Ruth's record for career home runs, but he had some big advantages. The season had been expanded by 8 games. Over Aaron's 23 season career that is an additional 184 games. An even more substantial advantage that Aaron had over Ruth was the designated hitter rule which allowed him to bat in games without playing in the field as he was finishing his career in the American League. This rule extended Aaron's career. And the ball itself had changed. It was arguably livelier by Aaron's time. Though Aaron was a great hitter, Aaron fans couldn't argue that Aaron was a better hitter than the Babe. Aaron's lifetime batting average was a hefty .305, but Ruth's was .342[20] The pitching was arguably more advanced in Aaron's time and, therefore, more difficult to hit. And Yankee Stadium, "the House that Ruth built," was actually more like the house that was built for Ruth. The right field corner was slightly less than 300 feet from home plate, the shortest fence in the major leagues, for the left-handed hitting Ruth. (Roger Maris was also a left- handed hitter, and this short fence contributed to his 61 home runs in 1961.)

Willie Mays retired before the designated hitter rule came into effect, but he still hit 660 home runs. He also maintained a high batting average. And he had a reputation as among the best centerfielders to ever play the game. Still he didn't show off;

---

[20] "Hank Aaron Stats," *Baseball Almanac*, http://www.baseball-almanac.com/players/player.php?p=aaronha01; Baseball Reference, http://www.baseball-reference.com/players/r/ruthba01.shtml

he played to win. His method for catching routine fly balls is still unique today. He caught them underhand with what is described as the "Willie Mays basket catch." The story behind this is that he was said to have misjudged at least one fly ball in his early career and had it go over his head. To make certain that this would never happen again, he invented the "basket catch" which allowed him a much greater margin of error.

Mays began his career for the Giants in New York. Then his Giants moved to San Francisco. This meant that his two home ballparks provided the most interesting challenges for a center fielder in all of the major leagues. The New York Giants did not play in a standard baseball park. They played in "the Polo Grounds." When the ball diamond was fitted to it, the deepest part of the centerfield was 483 feet from home plate, far deeper than in any other ballpark. This was the stage setting for "the catch" which Mays made in the eighth inning of game 1 of the 1954 World Series. The ball was hit deep to that deepest part of center field and Mays caught it on the run with his back to home plate. "The catch" prevented the opposing Cleveland Indians from scoring in the inning. The score remained tied and the Giants went on to win in extra innings. This "long out" would have been over the fence for a home run in any other park. "The catch" is still a famous moment in baseball history. After moving to San Francisco, the Giants played at Candle Stick Park near the ocean. The swirling winds were known to be problematic for outfielders, but Mays with his basket catch seemed to handle his position with ease anywhere.

The great shortstop Ernie Banks is too easily overlooked today because he played for one of the worst teams in the major leagues. But Banks, "Mr. Cub," was the first player ever selected as the Most Valuable Player in the National League two years in a row—1958-59. The fact that the Cubs had a losing record both those years makes the MVP honor for Banks all that much more remarkable. Banks would have been hard to pass over at that time. He hit a total of 92 home runs those two years, while playing shortstop, the most important defensive position on the field.[21] During his long career, Banks was selected for the All Star team 14 times and hit 512 home runs.

Stan Musial was one of the most consistent performers in the major leagues over a long period of time. He played his entire career

---

[21] Geoffrey C. Ward and Ken Burns, *Baseball: An Illustrated History,* (Alfred A. Knopf, Inc., 1994), p. 356.

for the St. Louis Cardinals and was selected for the National League All-Star team in 1943, 1944, and every year from 1946 through 1963. He was also selected as National League MVP three times. His 22 year career was interrupted with only a single one year hiatus in 1945, when he served in the US Navy in World War II. Musial's lifetime batting average was a hefty .331. He set several National League career hitting records, the most notable of which is most total hits at 3,630 (since broken by Pete Rose). I remember that he was known as a power hitter, batting in the cleanup position in the batting order (4th), and he was always considered a threat when he came to the plate. His home run career total was 475, and his 725 doubles was a National League record (also broken by Pete Rose). Throughout his long playing career, no one could think about the Cardinals without "Stan the Man."

The last of my baseball heroes whom I want to mention is Warren Spahn, the winningest left-handed pitcher in baseball history with 363 wins. This is made even more impressive because he interrupted his career to fight in World War II during which he fought in the Battle of the Bulge, received a Purple Heart, and was awarded a battlefield commission. He made up for his three season hiatus with amazing longevity. His career spanned 21 years. He was pitching well into his 40s. His baseball accolades included being selected for the All Star Team 14 times and leading the National League in number of wins for eight years, including five years in succession (1957 to 1961). Some of Spahn's numerous wins were helped by his own hitting ability. His batting average hovered around .200, almost as high as many position players. His teammate Bob Uecker could envy Spahn's hitting. (Uecker, a backup catcher his entire career, is a great baseball character who often pokes good-natured fun at himself as an announcer and author.)

My Milwaukee Braves were special in a strange way in 1961. They compiled impressive individual statistics while managing to achieve a mediocre won-lost record. They finished in fourth place in the eight team National League despite having four players who hit 25 or more home runs (Eddy Mathers, Hank Arron, Joe Adcock, and Frank Thomas[22]), four players who batted .300 or better (Mathers, Aaron, Thomas, and Frank Bowling), a twenty game winning pitcher (Warren Spahn at 21-13), and an 18 game winner (Lew

---

[22] This Frank Thomas is not to be confused with another player of the same name who came along later and is considerably more famous.

Burdette with a won-lost record of 18-11). They also had young Joe
Torre catching. He turned 20 that year and finished second in the
balloting for Rookie of the Year. What made these Braves even more
disappointing is that in the eight previous seasons since moving to
Milwaukee, the Braves had never finished lower than second place
while winning two league championships and one World Series.
Still they were fun and baseball was a great game. I attended my
first major league game that year in August. I saw Spahn pitch and
defeat the Pirates 2 to 1.[23]

Baseball was more than a spectator sport then. It was central
to the lives of millions of American boys. Many boys would get
together and play or practice without any adult supervision or
interference every day. We played both baseball and softball. In the
summertime, I often played in two such pick-up games in a day. I
had little natural talent, but by playing a lot I gradually got better.
I also learned a lot, most of which I learned too late to salvage my
baseball career. As a hitter, I learned to slow down my swing and
concentrate on hitting the ball on the head. You don't have to swing
hard; if you hit the ball squarely, it jumps off the bat. Swinging hard
did me no good at all. I also learned that when I was intimidated
by a strong pitcher, I always struck out. What I came to realize too
late was that the pitcher is irrelevant; when the ball is traveling
toward home plate the interaction is between the batter and the
ball. Forget the pitcher. The larger message I learned from all my
sports experience was that when I anticipated and feared failure,
I always failed, but if I anticipated success, I usually succeeded.

I always secretly wanted to be a pitcher. I did pitch in a few
games eventually. I learned to throw a curve ball. I also learned
that by using my fastball grip, throwing side arm, and flicking
my wrist on the delivery, I could run the ball in on a right-handed
batter in an intimidating way. I never perfected this pitch, but
it had potential. It was difficult for right-handed hitters because
the ball would be breaking toward the batter as he was swinging.
This would disrupt his timing. I have always thought that had I
continued to pitch in later years, I could work on this pitch and it
might just be the gimmick which I needed for a professional, albeit,
minor league, career. I still like to fantasize that this is among of

---

[23] The Milwaukee Braves were always an interesting team. In one
famous game in 1959, Pirate hurler, Harvey Haddox, pitched 12
perfect innings against them, only to lose in the 13th inning on
one hit.

the great "might have beens" in my life—a dream without a plan. As an educator I have heard many people preach to young people to "follow your dreams." This is simply not enough—think, plan, build your dreams, and the sooner you start, the better.

The lessons I learned about success from playing sports can serve anyone well in any endeavor. Planning and preparation are prerequisite for success. For best results focus, concentrate, be in the moment. Expect to succeed and you will probably succeed; expect to fail and you will fail. Teamwork makes everyone perform better and feel better about the effort, and your teammates will perform better if you express confidence in them. Of course you might get to the major leagues in the same way you can get to Carnegie Hall, "Practice, practice, practice." The great football coach Vince Lombardi who was known to be a proponent of hard work famously said, "The only place success comes before work is in the dictionary."[24]

I must also admit that I learned some bad habits from baseball and resisted some others. Arguing with the umpire was modeled by major league baseball managers and coaches. It seemed to be something that one was expected to do. I see coaches today continuing to act this way. I don't think it reflects well on them, and it teaches young people to be unreasonable, demanding, and disrespectful. Sports officials do a difficult, demanding job which is often thankless. The other bad habit being modeled by baseball players was chewing tobacco. I'm happy that that never appealed to me. It can cause mouth cancer. We once had a former minor league baseball player, who was deformed with half his jaw missing, come to a school at which I was teaching to talk about his use of chewing tobacco.

As an adult, I haven't played much ball. When I have played softball, the wonder of the game was still with me. The baseball diamond is a magical place where I can forget about all plans and all problems and be totally in the moment. Only the game matters. Concentration is only on the ball. When I'm hitting, only the ball and I exist. (The bat is just an extension of me). Every play is an opportunity. Life could not be simpler or more beautiful. I know that this is the appeal of all sports. I can get close to the same feeling playing tennis, but baseball is just more personal to me.

Jim Bouton, a good pitcher who had lost his fastball, was

---

[24] Lombardi, Vince, contained in *Brainy Quote*
https://www.brainyquote.com/quotes/vince_lombardi_109282

attempting to make a comeback by specializing as a knuckleball pitcher in 1969, when he wrote *Ball Four*, a journal of his experiences and thoughts during that season. In the last sentence of that book, he perfectly encapsulates what baseball meant to many boomers in the 60s by saying, "You spend a good piece of your life gripping a baseball and in the end it turns out that it was the other way around all the time."

Camelot and the New Frontier

In the summer of 1960, the US was on the verge of a big change. America's oldest president up to that time, Republican Dwight D. Eisenhower, was in the last year of his second term. He would be replaced by America's second youngest president, a Democrat. Eisenhower had provided my first great disillusionment that May when he forcefully denied that America was sending spy planes over the Soviet Union, only to be embarrassed when Soviet Premiere Nikita Khrushchev produced a captured pilot. Our president lied. I was 11 and I was shocked.

That 1960 presidential election pitted the handsome, glamorous, navy war hero, John Kennedy, against the less colorful US Vice-president, Richard Nixon, who was, himself, also a World War II Navy veteran. Kennedy was a Catholic. We would think nothing about that today, but then people were worried that he would be controlled by the Pope. The highlights of the campaign were four televised debates. This was the beginning of the tradition of televised presidential debates. When polled, most people who watched the debates said that Kennedy won, but those who listened to the debates on the radio generally gave the edge to Nixon. The election was extremely close. Kennedy won the popular vote by less than 100,000. He also narrowly won the electoral vote. To win Illinois he needed to win in Chicago. Chicago Mayor Richard Daley came through, though some people speculated about voter fraud saying that dead people pushed Kennedy over the top in the windy city. Kennedy quipped privately after the election that if he never did anything else, he had at least saved America from Richard Nixon.

The American era of Camelot began on a bitterly cold day in Washington, DC, January 20, 1961. Heavy snow the night before had caused some flight cancellations and made clearing the way for the inauguration difficult. Kennedy challenged Americans to national service saying famously, "Ask not what your country can do for you; ask what you can do for your country." He soon created the Peace Corps by executive order, and it is still in existence today doing good work all over the world. The young president also directed the country to look to the "New Frontier" with a bold proposal: to send a man to the moon and return him safely to earth by the end of the decade, even though the technology to do this did not yet exist then, and America was still behind in the space race.[25] Nevertheless, the goal would be reached with Neil Armstrong's lunar stroll in 1969. In February 1962, John Glenn orbited the earth, and America took the lead in the space race never to relinquish that lead again. America could do anything by applying American brain power, and America could make the world better. The image of the American Camelot was further enhanced by John Kennedy's beautiful, sophisticated wife, Jaqueline, two beautiful children, and the "brain trust" cabinet with many of its members selected from top US universities. America was a country excited and on the move.

With Kennedy, Americans were feeling a closer connection to their president than had been the case with Eisenhower. Kennedy held regular press conferences which were televised. At first, many people watched these because they were informative. Then people continued to watch because these press conferences were also entertaining. The banter was lively and the President was cleaver and engaging. Kennedy also addressed the nation in speeches from the Oval Office on important issues of national concern, civil rights being one of those concerns. Jacqueline Kennedy gave a televised White House tour. Impressionist Vaughn Meader produced a humorous record album gently poking good-natured fun at *The First Family*. It sold 2.5 million copies in its first month, making it the fastest-selling album in history at that time. It went on to sell 7 million copies and won a Grammy for album of the year.[26] First family pictures inside and outside the White House were common in American magazines. Many people had a picture of the President displayed prominently in their homes and workplaces, especially the Catholic families. America was experiencing a romance with

---

[25] Soviet cosmonaut Yuri Gagarin would become the first man in space in April 1961.

[26] McLellen, Dennis, "Vaughn Meader, 68; Comedian Known for Impersonating JFK," *Los Angeles Times,* October 30, 2004

John Kennedy and his family even as the President wrestled with huge challenges both domestically and internationally.

Mainstream American culture appeared to be becoming more vibrant and colorful in these early 1960s. *Bonanza* had premiered in 1959 in full color from its very beginning with the goal of selling color televisions to America. American fascination with outer space spawned the popular *Outer Limits* television series, which ran between 1963 and 1965. Chubby Checker was teaching us to do the twist, while Dick Clark was also encouraging us to dance with his *American Bandstand.* The intended demographic for *Bandstand* was the teenager, but I think that I was more like the typical fan. I love it at a certain age, but I had outgrown it by the time I was about twelve.

Music inspired by the folk tradition and with more serious themes was beginning to catch on by the Camelot years. Peter, Paul, and Mary asked "Where Have All the Flowers Gone?" a song written by Pete Seeger in 1955 finally finding its time. I preferred the Kingston Trio, who also recorded a version of the same song. The exciting new talent in the folk genre was Bob Dylan. His first big album, *The Free Wheelin' Bob Dylan,* was released in May 1963. Mitch Miller was getting families to *Sing Along with Mitch.* The disaffected college age crowd, labelled "beatniks" were writing poetry in Greenwich Village and other places, but not in my town. And hemlines were rising, something I watched with interest as I was entering puberty.

The optimism of Camelot was challenged internally by a deep racial divide which the younger generations today might have difficulty imagining. Segregation and inequality were common in the north, as well as in the south. In the south, the inequality was more likely to be official and formalized in laws. African-Americans were demanding equality. Like other minority groups, African-Americans had served honorably in World War II, and some, like the Tuskegee Airmen, had won great distinction. The time to end discrimination was long overdue. I knew this, but there was only one black person that I knew of in my entire town of 32,000. It was easy for people like me to say that segregation was wrong, but I lived in a whole different world it seemed, completely segregated.

African-Americans will see the progress made on civil rights issues in the 1960s differently than I. That does not mean that they are wrong or that I am wrong, but we do see the world through different lenses. However, all of America was seeing the ugliness of southern racism through the television news cameras in the early 1960s. Network news teams were exposing what had not been exposed before on a daily basis. The changes I saw in the 60s appeared to me to be tremendous, almost miraculous progress in race relations and equal justice, even though we still had much to do to achieve a color-blind society. Some African-Americans understandably disagree with this assessment.

I can say two things for certain about the Civil Rights Movement of the 1960s. First, it was not a single unified movement. It was lots of people, mostly African-Americans, doing lots of things. Everyone knows about Martin Luther King, Jr. and the Southern Christian Leadership Conference, and rightfully reveres King for his efforts. But the NAACP (National Association for the Advancement of Colored People) has been actively striving for racial equality since its founding by W.E.B. DuBois in 1909. There were also newly formed organizations like SNCC, the Students Nonviolence Coordinating Committee, which was organizing "sitting-ins" to desegregate lunch counters. CORE, the Congress of Racial Equality, led by James Farmer, was engaged in "freedom rides" to desegregate bus transportation. Malcolm X with the Nations of Islam was standing up with a different philosophy, promising to meet violence with violence. Eldridge Clever and the Black Panthers were even more militant in defense of African-Americans.

The second thing I can say about this multifaceted movement is that America is a better place for all of us today because of the Civil Rights Movement. There is no justice or peace in an unjust society. Few people in 1955 could have imagined the tremendous strides toward equality which our society was to make and how our society would be changed by 1980. The great inhibitor of progress is the shortsighted belief that what has always been will always be. If what has always been is morally wrong, it needs to be aggressively challenged in order to create a new, more just paradigm.

The need for civil rights reform was not the only urgent issue confronting Camelot. The Cold War was at its height and the danger was near. In 1959 the revolutionary, Fidel Castro, had seized power in Cuba, soon after declaring himself an ally of the Soviet Union. The one odd thing that I remember about this is that in the beginning Americans weren't sure about whether Castro was a hero or a villain, whether he was a democrat (small "d") or a communist. When it became certain where Castro stood, the CIA began training Cuban exiles in Florida to retake the island. A plot was formed by the CIA during Eisenhower's last year; Kennedy inherited it. When that plot was put into motion, the American trained counterrevolutionaries seemed to have expected American air support for their landing in Cuba. They got only a token attack by US B-52 bombers on Cuban airfields the night before the invasion. Without air cover, the entire force was quickly captured or killed. Kennedy came on the television to announce what had happened to the American people and claimed full personal responsibility for the failure. He had been president for only three months at that time.

Of course the major Cuban challenge to Kennedy and the brain trust was the Cuban Missile Crisis in October 1962. This is the time when the world was closer to nuclear war than it ever had been or would be (at least up to now). Soviet missiles capable of delivering nuclear warheads to the United States were detected in Cuba. Some of America's top military leaders advocated invasion of Cuba, but this would have brought the Soviet Union into a war with the US. President Kennedy moved slowly and with deliberation. Robert Kennedy, the president's brother who was the attorney general, became a key advisor in the strategic discussions. The Kennedys (John and Robert) agreed on a "quarantine" of Cuba. This was a blockade by another name. They did not call this a blockade, because a blockade is an act of war. Soviet Premier Nikita Khrushchev did call it an illegal blockade, but stopped short of calling it an act of war.

People all over the US were following the drama closely. In Wisconsin, where I was, people seemed very interested but not overly concerned. Our cows and our breweries would not have been high priority targets for nuclear attack, and war did not seem to be likely yet. The Cold War had been a fact of life since before I was born. My generation knew nothing else. The fact that a major US-Soviet war had not yet occurred gave reason to believe that one would not occur now. If war did occur, it would seem to have been only natural, the condition of the world. The history of western civilization up to that time seemed to me to be the story of perpetual war punctuated with intermittent peace. This was especially true of the twentieth century. If any trend existed, it was toward more wars in my time.

Fortunately, at the critical juncture of October 1962, both Kennedy and Khrushchev determined to affect history rather than be effected by it. To do this they needed to make a deal. Nuclear war was not an option. Khrushchev was not Stalin; Khrushchev could be brash and aggressive at times, but he understood the gravity of the nuclear age. In his own way, he was trying to do the best for his country and the world. Kennedy and Khrushchev agreed that the Soviets would remove the missiles from Cuba, and the US would promise never to invade Cuba. This much was made public. What was not publicized at the time was a secret agreement Kennedy made to remove US missiles which could strike the Soviet Union from Turkey. Khrushchev allowed Kennedy to keep this secret and appear strong even though without this concession he (Khrushchev) appeared weak at home.

The quarantine was lifted. An American embargo of Cuba would continue for decades and the CIA would continue to plot Castro's assassination, but the Cuban threat was permanently ended.[27] As much as Kennedy can be praised for his handling of Cuba then, he should also be criticized for his mishandling of Vietnam. Like US-Cuban involvement, our involvement in Vietnam had begun under President Eisenhower. Ike had committed the US to help South Vietnam. This was the first in a long series of errors by men who were blind to reality, and Kennedy was one of those blind men.

After the Japanese occupation of Vietnam during World War II, the French had attempted to reestablish their Vietnam colony. They were opposed by forces under the nationalist/communist, Ho Chi Minh, who had declared the independence of Vietnam. A revolutionary war ensued which ended with French defeat in 1954. At that time, a struggle for power and leadership resulted in a brief civil war, which ended with a compromise. Vietnam was to be temporarily divided at the 17th parallel. The north was to be communist under Ho Chi Minh. The south would be capitalist under Ngo Dinh Diem. This was to be only temporary. A date was set by which elections were to be held to reunify the country. When that date was reached, Diem declared South Vietnam to be independent, refusing to hold the election as promised, and appealing for help from the United States.

In the beginning, America was providing funds, arms, equipment, and military advisors. By 1962 it was becoming increasingly obvious that the South Vietnamese army was losing the war. This is when the 15,000 US soldiers and airmen in Vietnam at that time were quietly becoming involved in combat, first with air support, then with limited ground operations still in a mostly supporting role. This

---

[27] Among the many CIA assassination plots is one which envisioned the use of an exploding cigar.

was illegal without a declaration of war or the consent of Congress at that time, but Congress took no action to correct the situation and no court challenges surfaced. By the following year, protests on the streets of Saigon were indicating that the Diem government lacked popular support. The most spectacular event among these protests occurred when a Buddhist monk burned himself to death in the center of the city before the television cameras. We saw this that night on the evening news in the US. This was the first time I thought to myself, *Something is wrong in Vietnam.* I was just 14 years old. The adults must have at least considered this.

But the entire American society failed to attend to the self-immolation. The news media did not follow-up with probing questions. The Kennedy administration did not appear to take any strong actions, or even make any statements about the event. Congress continued to be absent from any discussion of Vietnam. No voice of moral outcry was heard from any opinion leaders—religious or secular. The moral fiber of America was totally poisoned by the Cold War. As bad as Soviet Communism was, fear of communism had turned America into much of what we feared—a police state, which discouraged dissenting opinion, and a sponsor of international suppression. The Saigon incident quickly faded from the spotlight and Kennedy remained popular.

Kennedy's fortunes continued to rise. Khrushchev's situation, on the other hand, was turning negative. During that last Kennedy year, a movement was begun in the secrecy of the Kremlin to remove Khrushchev from power for his appearance of weakness. Cuba and Vietnam had not been the only communist challenges to Kennedy. In 1961 Khrushchev ordered construction of the Berlin Wall. In the first months of the Wall, we witnessed on television East Berliners dying on the Wall, caught in the barbed wire and shot by guards. This was embarrassing for President Kennedy and required intelligent constraint because American action here would have brought on war with the colossal Soviet land army which was in position to go at a moment's notice. From the Soviet point of view the Wall was a near necessity to contain the "brain drain" of skilled professionals fleeing to a better life in the west. When Khrushchev allowed Kennedy to look good in 1962, this may have been to help a partner in the peace process who appeared weak because of the Wall and the Bay of Pigs failure. Kennedy and Khrushchev were about to negotiate the first major power nuclear test ban treaty the following year, and Kennedy needed to appear strong in order to be able to shepherd it through Congress. Earlier that summer, Kennedy went to Berlin and made a speech at the Wall, pledging American support and solidarity with the people of West Berlin.

Congress ratified the treaty, and John Kennedy, learning from his experiences, was showing the potential to become one of America's great presidents, though we have no way of knowing where his Vietnam policy would have gone. He had not yet made a deep commitment to Vietnam. Martin Luther King pressured him for greater support of civil rights reform throughout his presidency, and he responded with Justice Department efforts to protect civil rights demonstrators under the direction of Attorney General Robert Kennedy and speeches from the Oval Office appealing to all Americans to support racial justice. One could argue that Kennedy could have done more for civil rights, but he did speak out forcefully on more than one occasion and defined himself to be on the side of equal justice. Dr. King led his march on Washington in the summer of 1963 and gave his famous "I Have a Dream" speech. Kennedy planned to respond with a sweeping civil rights bill to move the country forward. But before the President could sell his civil rights bill to Congress, he went to Dallas, Texas.

Friday, November 22 was a clear, fairly warm day in Dallas. John and Jackie Kennedy road in the back of a top down convertible. An assassin who appears to have been a deranged opportunist did the unimaginable. It has often been said that everyone remembers that day. I can confirm that I do. I was in ninth grade. Right after lunch I was in study hall when the intercom came on announcing that we would be listening to the news of an important event. Then the news of the shooting came on. The announcer said that the President had been shot in the head and at least part of his brain was blown out. He had been taken to the hospital. All that afternoon, we didn't do anything in school except to listen to the radio. The bells rang and we changed classes, but we just sat and quietly listened to the radio. There wasn't much of the usual noise in the hall at passing time. We walked pretty quietly, in shock. That evening I saw Walter Cronkite, the famous CBS news anchorman, choking back tears as he announced Kennedy's death. We had off school on Monday, the day of the funeral; it was declared a national day of mourning. Camelot had ended abruptly.

High School and the Great Society

Conspiracy theories abound regarding the Kennedy assassination, not completely without reason. Lee Harvey Oswald, the assassin, had at one time attempted to defect to the Soviet Union. Soon after the assassination, Oswald was captured and held in jail in Dallas, but before he could be thoroughly interrogated, he was, himself, assassinated with a small handgun while being transferred in police custody two days later. That event was caught on live TV. That assassin, Jack Ruby, was a Dallas nightclub owner who had been, to some extent, involved with organized crime. Ruby was tried for the murder of Oswald and sentenced to death. On appeal, Ruby was to be granted a new trial some years later. Just before that trial was to take place Ruby died of pulmonary embolism associated with lung cancer. Another twist in the mystery is that the president of South Vietnam, Ngo Dinh Diem, had been assassinated less than three weeks before the Kennedy assassination, supposedly with the blessing of the CIA. The administration's policy with regard to the Vietnam War would logically have been under reconsideration at that time. Kennedy was killed before he could formulate and announce a new Vietnam policy. A government commission, headed by the Chief Justice of the Supreme Court, Earl Warren, and including Congressman Gerald Ford, was formed to investigate Kennedy's assassination. That commission compiled multiple volumes of information and testimony only to conclude that Oswald had acted alone, though some of the evidence suggested another shooter. People still do not want to believe that one deranged young man could suddenly find himself with the opportunity to kill a president. So, who killed Kennedy? Some said the CIA; some said organized crime; or perhaps the Russians? Could this have been a prelude to an invasion?

An apparently unrelated invasion did, in fact, occur less than three months later. To great fanfare, the Beatles landed in New York to spearhead the British invasion. America had a new diversion. The Brits quickly took over the American popular music scene, bringing excitingly fresh vitality. The Rolling Stones followed the Beatles and America's young were hooked. The UK clearly took the lead in rock music in the mid-1960s. The Rolling Stones released their first "Big Hits" album in 1966, and I don't think they ever made a better album. "Satisfaction" and "Nineteenth Nervous Breakdown" and "Time is on My Side" and "Heart of Stone"—these songs set a standard that no one, not even the Beatles, ever reached again. The Animals were another of my favorites British groups with songs like "We Gotta Get Outta This Place" (if it's the last thing we ever do). The Animals also did a haunting rendition of the old folk song, "House of the Rising Sun," which rose to number one on the charts in both England and the US in 1964.

The American answer to this British invasion was Motown, contributing powerful, uniquely American music. The Supremes with Dianna Ross was the top Motown group. They were 17 year old high school girls when they began recording for Motown. Two other Motown girl groups, which coincidentally also began as schoolmates, are also worth mentioning. These are The Chiffons and my personal favorites, The Shirelles. Some of the biggest Motown names were Smoky Robinson, Percy Sledge, Aretha Franklin, Gladys Knight, and The Four Tops. The incredible "Little" Stevie Wonder was eleven years old when he began his career with Motown. People were passionate about the music of the time. This was the swinging 60s. Hemlines continued to rise. Perhaps the sky was the limit.

The big news in the sporting world was that the young Cassius Clay defeated Sonny Liston to become heavyweight boxing champion of the world. Clay had won a gold medal at the 1960 Olympics, but he had been somewhat unimpressive in his early professional career. No one expected that he was ready to challenge the great Sonny Liston who had twice dispatched the previous heavyweight champion, Floyd Patterson, easily with first round knockouts. In the first Liston-Clay meeting in February 1964, Liston failed to answer the bell for the eighth round. When the rematch occurred in May 1965, the fight was televised nationally. It was not much of a fight. Clay knocked out Liston in the second round. Liston went down so easily that many people suspected that he may have taken a dive. It is possible that Sonny Liston figured that he could not defeat Clay, but he could collect one more big check in his career just by getting into the ring.

Cassius Clay soon changed his name to Muhammad Ali and declared that he was Muslim. He was part of America's "Black Muslim" movement which rejected Christianity as the religion of the white oppressors and embraced Islam as the religion of independent African-Americans (conveniently forgetting that Arabs who brought Islam to Sub-Sahara Africa were slave traders). Ali, himself, was bold, loud, and boastful. He constituted an entirely new cultural phenomena which many African-Americans embraced, and he brazenly reminded America of the urgent need to address its racial problems.

America's new president intended to do just that, but he had only one year remaining before the next election. Lyndon Baines Johnson was running for reelection almost as soon as he took office. His opponent was Arizona Senator Barry Goldwater. The issue that defined the 1964 campaign was the Vietnam War. The US had become involved in Vietnam because of the domino theory. The communists had defeated the nationalist in China in 1949. Communist aggression had been stopped in South Korea in 1953 at great cost, but now communism was on the move in Southeast Asia. It was believed that if communism succeeded in Vietnam all of South Asia would be threatened. Communists were already gaining a foothold in neighboring Laos. A common fallacy was that all "communist aggression" was directed by the Soviet Union or China, as if people in other countries could not think for themselves. This is why American leaders did not see Ho Chi Minh as a true nationalist or Ngo Diem as a dictator lacking popular support. While the commitment to South Vietnam begun under Eisenhower was not unlimited under Kennedy, and Kennedy may have been considering ending or reducing that commitment, both Lyndon Johnson and Barry Goldwater could only see Vietnam in the context of the Cold War and the domino theory.

Goldwater campaigned on winning the war at whatever cost. He was labeled an extremist and readily accepted that charge saying famously, "Extremism in defense of liberty is no vice."[28] He also frightened many Americans by calling the atomic bomb just another weapon. Polling showed that most Americans disagreed with Goldwater. The Republican Party could only hope that support for aggressive militarism was more widespread than polls indicated but most Americans did not want to admit this support in public. The Goldwater campaign slogan became, "In your heart you know he's right." Johnson played the moderate to Goldwater's extremism and won the election by a landslide. Helped also by a strong sympathy vote for Kennedy's unfinished agenda, Johnson carried 44 states and pulled a strong Democratic majority into Congress on his long coattails.

What followed in the Johnson years was a giant leap forward--"the

---

[28] Goldwater, Barry, in acceptance speech for the Presidential nomination to the Republican National Convention in The Cow Palace, San Francisco, July 16, 1964.

Great Society" programs. These encompassed "the War on Poverty," civil rights reform, early environmentalism, and support for the arts. The "War on Poverty", which Johnson had announced in his State of the Union Address in January 1965, was the most ambitious component of the Great Society. An Office of Economic Opportunity was created to oversee a myriad of programs—Job Corps, VISTA, Head Start, Work-Study, and others. Job Corps provided vocational training to disadvantaged youth. VISTA was a domestic version of the Peace Corps which attempted to get volunteer teachers into schools in impoverished communities. Head Start provided early education opportunities and nutrition to children living in poverty. And the work-study program provided federal funds for colleges to employ financially needy students. The crowning, and most lasting achievements of President Johnson's War on Poverty were Medicare and Medicaid.

The historic 1964 Civil Rights Act had actually been proposed by Johnson and passed before the election. It outlawed racially discriminatory hiring practices and segregated public accommodations, including all retail establishments, restaurants, etc. The new Democratic majority in Congress followed it up with the Voting Rights Act of 1965, which outlawed the "literacy tests" which many southern states had used to restrict African-Americans from voting. The law also had a provision which specified that changes in voting regulations would be subject to federal approval in certain districts or states which had a history of discriminatory practices. These two monumental laws were the tipping point in the Civil Rights Movement and race relations in the US, and, as Lyndon Johnson, a Texan, liked to remind his fellow Americans, they were both directly attributable to a president from the south.

President Johnson seems to have had as a goal a complete remaking of the American society. A Water Quality Act (1965) and a Clean Air Restoration Act (1966) were passed early in his administration, before the environmental movement of the 1970s had begun. The National Endowment for the Arts was created and with it, PBS (Public Broadcasting System television) and NPR (National Public Radio) were born. The President's "Great Society" was, in most ways, a great success. If Lyndon Johnson had done nothing else, he might be remembered today as one America's greatest presidents.

Unfortunately, rapid and extensive escalation of the Vietnam War became what the Johnson years are most known for today.

Once reelected, Johnson removed his cloak of moderation and began sending large numbers of combat troops to Vietnam. Congress had passed the Gulf of Tonkin Resolution in August 1964, which gave the President a free hand to run the war in any way he wished without Congressional oversight. The number of US troops in Vietnam increased to over half a million by 1968, but the war seemed unwinnable. This was the first war to be included in the everyday television news, and it was in full horrific color. The number of American dead continued to mount, and President Johnson agonized over why so many young Americans seemed to hate him, despite all the good he was bringing with the Great Society. Young people were often chanting at demonstrations outside the White House "Hey, hey, LBJ, how many kids did you kill today?" but LBJ didn't want to hear it. As early as 1964 there was a growing undercurrent of discontent in America, due mainly to the war. This is perhaps best illustrated by three iconic songs of the era: "The Times They are A-Changin'" (1964) by Bob Dylan, "The Eve of Destruction" (1965) by Barry McGuire, and "For What It's Worth" (1967) by Buffalo Springfield.

My high school friends and I were aware of the issues of our time, of course, but we were not particularly among the disaffected yet. We didn't really hate the president then. We didn't think much about him. We lived our own little lives in our own little world as teenagers do. My biggest concern was getting a driver's license. Dances, high school football and basketball games, our own little touch football and basketball games, movies, "tooling the gut" (driving up and down Main Street), bowling, and just hanging out, these were the inane activities which occupied our time. We were all interested in cars and some of us were also interested in motorbikes. There was a motorbike craze in the mid-1960s. Honda was among the most popular brands of these small motorcycles. Their engine sizes generally ran from 50cc to 350cc. They had a smart advertisement campaign with the catchy slogan, "You meet the nicest people on a Honda." I got my first real job when I was 16 and purchased a "nifty-fifty", Honda 50 cc, which was lots fun.

I was losing interest in baseball as a spectator sport; football had more appeal. Journalist Mary McGrory made an astute observation when she said, "Baseball is what we were, football is what we have become."[29] The 1960s was the decade of transition and the Green Bay Packers stood tall above all other professional football teams that decade. Nearly everyone in my home state of Wisconsin was, and still is, a Packers fan. The Packers, under Coach Vince Lombardi, began their incredible streak with the Western Conference Championship of the NFL in 1960, but the Packers lost in the league championship game to Philadelphia. Then in 1961 the Packers repeated as conference champions and won their first league championship of the 1960s by defeating the Eastern Conference Champion New York Giants 37-0. The following year the Packers won it all again. Their next league championship was in 1965. This was the first of three in a row. When the NFL merged with the AFL and the Super Bowl was begun, the Packers won the first two easily. That is why the Super Bowl trophy is called the Lombardi Trophy. The Packers of the 1960s matter because they achieved excellence by dedication through team effort. In the years of the three straight NLF championships (and first two Super Bowls), 1965-1967, the Packers had only three standout players, the great linebacker Ray Nitschke, fullback Jim Taylor, and running/passing/kicking sensation Paul Hornung. Certainly none who were bellicose the way players are today. Hornung was suspended for the 1963 season for gambling and forced out of football by injuries after the 1966 season in which he had limited playing time. One crucial element to the Packers success was a tremendous blocking line. A number of running backs other than Taylor and Hornung looked like superstars when running behind that Packer line, and the team always seemed to be better as a team than the sum of the parts. Lombardi was a truly inspirational coach.

I should mention that I am an only child raised by grandparents. That's why I do not write about any siblings. My unimpressive high school career is only worth mentioning for what it says about motivation. My grandparents had very low expectations for me after my dismal start in elementary school. The comment with which my report card was always met was "Well, at least you passed" (remembering that I hadn't in second grade). I remember that as I began my sophomore year I had a few classes in which I was genuinely interested, and I decided to make an effort in school. I proudly brought home a report card with 3 "A"s and 3 "B"s (the

---

[29] McGrory, Mary. Contained in *The Best Things Anybody Ever Said*, ed. Robert Byrne New York: Touchstone, 2014) #2304.

best I ever did in high school). My grandmother looked at it and said, "Well, at least you passed." I slid back to my old attitude of "Who cares?" To be fair, my grandparents did buy me books, when I was in elementary school. The books they bought were attractive, with interesting pictures and beautiful maps which stimulated my interest in learning. My high school teachers, however, provided the motivation which set the direction of my life. They must have colluded cleverly. They did not ask me, "Are you planning to go to college?" Instead they asked, "**Where** are you planning to go to college?" With this question, they set a definite expectation in my mind; I was definitely going to college. I didn't know how I was going to finance it. I knew that I was not going to ask my grandparents to help. I would work my way through somehow.

I became, like most boys, a partial achiever. I wanted to do well enough in school to qualify for college and for some undefined, unknown success in the future. But I didn't want to stand out as someone who was trying his hardest. So, I missed lots of opportunities—opportunities for intrinsic growth and external reward, and probably some career possibilities. One of the worst misnomers I have ever heard is the term "overachiever." It is a poor descriptor and often used by students as an excuse for laziness. There are partial achievers like me; there are underachievers; and there are achievers.

Those students who insist that they have to get all "A" grades, are focusing on the wrong goal. The goal should be knowledge, not "A's". Because grades have become so inflated today, students would do much better to concentrate their efforts on being able to achieve a high SAT score, rather than high grades. Extra-curricular activities and community involvement are also important factors that colleges are looking at today in terms of admissions and scholarships. Many students who feel pressured to get all "A's" become anxious and depressed. These are the students who are commonly labeled "overachievers." I think that if we have to label these students, "overachievers" is not a good term, because it disparages achievement as something unhealthy. It's funny that if a boy obsesses on athletic achievement, we say "He is dedicated," but if he puts the same energy into academics, we worry that the interest may be unhealthy. While teaching in the Peace Corps in Jordan, I noticed that many of my students (all boys) approached their studies with the same enthusiasm as American boys approach athletics. These students do better than American students, and will always do better, not because their schools are better, but because they are better students—they are achievers.

Entering the Adult World

High School ended for me in June of 1967, and two weeks later I was in an aluminum tube high above the ground headed into my future. There was no security screening at the airport at that time. Anyone could walk right up to the gates to see a friend off or meet him as he got off the plane. We had an inflight meal with regular silverware, and the meal included a pack of three cigarettes. After the meal everyone lit up. I did too. After all, the cigarettes were free. I was flying to a faraway place, Fort Polk, Louisiana, to embark on my first adult adventure. I don't believe that I had ever been out of Wisconsin, nor more than 100 miles from my home before that, and I had been away from home overnight only twice. Now I was on my way to the army. I remember that during my first week in the army I would wake up in the middle of the night and look around and think, *Where the hell am I?* Then I would remember, *Oh, shit! I'm in the army,* and I would lay back down and go back to sleep.

The Vietnam War was at its height then and the draft was extensive. So, every young man had to choose a path. You could wait to be drafted; you could enlist (4 years if you chose the safer option of air force or the navy); you could flee to Canada; you could claim to be a conscientious objector; or you could go to college and get a temporary deferment. When Uncle Sam got you, you would very likely go to Vietnam for a year where the chances of dying, dying for nothing, were formidable. Many young men chose college. Some went to Canada. Many guys waited to be drafted. Most got their notices around their nineteenth birthday.

Muhammad Ali claimed conscientious objector status and faced a long court battle which he eventually won. However, the boxing commission stripped him of his title and refused to allow him to box while his case was under review. He wouldn't fight overseas, so he wouldn't be allowed to fight in America. Ali's claim was upheld in 1971 and he was again allowed to box at age 29, having missed the years of his prime. He wasn't the same athlete he had been, but he was smarter. By fighting smarter and with enormous courage, Muhammad Ali fought all the leading heavyweight contenders over the next several years. He began by fighting Joe Frazier, the then reigning world heavyweight champion. Ali lost by decision, a decision which could easily have gone the other way. He later won a rematch with Frazier, but Frazier had already lost the championship to George Foreman. In 1974 Ali defeated Foreman to regain the championship and his career continued after that.

Ali had always been a champion for African-Americans. By the end of his career he had elevated his status with his own courage and dignity. His demeanor was not the same as it had been when he was young. He had grown tremendously though he was still loud and bold. He continued to be a man of dignity in his retirement as he coped with his boxing induced Parkinson's disease. His is a great American success story. He was a legitimate conscientious objector to the Vietnam War.

Besides the fact that the war seemed to be morally wrong, the demand for service was extremely discriminatory. This was "a rich man's war and a poor man's fight." A young man who wanted to get out of service and could afford tuition could go to college and have at least four years of deferment, during which he could hope for an end to the war. There was also a backdoor route out for some with connections, the National Guard or the Army Reserve. The average man could not get into these organization. They were full, but someone with connections could get in (George W. Bush got in.), and these organizations were not being called to active duty.

The war was troubling to everyone's conscience. But I was not a conscientious objector, nor was I from a rich family. I enlisted to get it over with and move forward with veteran's benefits (if I lived). As a young man, it was easy for me to have a cavalier attitude toward my own mortality. Most young men think that they are indestructible until faced with eminent danger. I never had to face such danger. Through dumb luck and standing in the wrong line at the right time, I survived without going to Vietnam, and I served an undistinguished hitch, all in the United States. I know that service in the military is life changing for many, but for me it was not. I can't honestly say that I gained any life lessons from the military. I did learn to fire a variety of weapons—the M-14 and M-16 rifles, a 45 caliber pistol and a 45 submachinegun, a 30 mm machinegun and 50 mm machinegun with tracer rounds, and the main gun of a tank. I had never fired a weapon before, and I have not fired one since. I was a lousy shot with the rifles at first, because I expected to be. I got better when I changed my expectation. But this is a lesson I had already learned through baseball.

Shooting and driving were the unique experiences the military provided me. I was privileged to have driven a jeep, a large truck, and a tank. I even drove a farm tractor in the army when I was briefly assigned to cutting grass. With the extra weight of the grass cutter attached, I could pop little wheelies. Like everyone else, I complained about the army while I was in, but looking back at it now, I was lucky and I had fun. I would like to say that I learned respect and patriotism, but the army then was under the severe stress of the Vietnam War. I did not respect the army as it was then, and many others with whom I served felt the same way.

I am happy to say that I was so stubborn that the army was unable to teach me to smoke. Smoking was nearly mandatory in the army at that time. In training we would have a 10 minute break every hour, during which we were often required to stay in formation—but we were encouraged to smoke—"Light em' up." So, one hundred ninety-nine guys lit up, and I stood somewhere in the cloud of smoke without a cigarette. This was not a health or moral stand, but a practical idea. We cleared about $70 a month as recruits. All those guys who were smoking the normal two packs a day were spending 80 cent per day on cigarettes. This was $24 a month—one-third of their pay. I thought *I can buy lots of beer with that money.* Years later I was not battling addiction to nicotine, as all those other guys were, and I'm still alive today with healthy lungs. (My beer belly is manageable, too.) I find it amusing that the military today tries to discourage smoking among its soldiers.

When I completed my hitch in the army, I took my GI Bill to college where I studied economics, history, and cheap wines while majoring in fun. I was a less than serious student. (Pagan Pink Ripple was my favorite go-to wine, but Boones Farm and Spanada were okay too.) I had not yet fully learned that you get out of any experience in proportion to what you put into it. If I had been a serious student, I could have opened some doors for myself, and I might have led a more useful life. Unfortunately for me, I would not begin to become a serious student until years later, when I began graduate school. My advice to a young person entering college today would be to open every door while you have the chance. Unopened doors can be difficult to open later on. As a student, be a professional.

While I was in college, I discovered *Star Trek*. The series had run in the mid-1960s for two and a half seasons and been abruptly cancelled by the network. In the early 1970s it was reborn in syndication and caught on, especially among young college students. I became a lifelong *Trekkie*. The main appeal of *Star Trek*, the original series, is the lively interaction between the three main characters, but it also has appeal in that it throws light on social issues. One *Star Trek* episode featured the first televised interracial kiss. Kirk and Uhura were forced to kiss, and the way it was portrayed, one would think that they were each fearful of contracting some deadly disease from the experience. *Star Trek's* creator, Gene Roddenberry, was deliberately breaking new ground. In its time, as the crew explored new worlds, *Star Trek* represented the possibility of a better world here, on earth.

There were two other television shows of the early 70s which also became popular while exposing social problems. These were the breakthrough comedies, *All in the Family* and *MASH*. *All in the Family* exposed the faulty logic of the lead character Archie Bunker, who was racist without really meaning any harm to anyone or having any self-awareness that his attitudes could be offensive. We all knew people like Archie. My grandmother was funny that way. I remember her saying more than once: "I worked with the N... women in the laundry in Milwaukee, and some of the N... was just as good as some of the whites." What *All in the Family* did was to help awaken people to just how common and wrong these attitudes were.

MASH offered more sophisticated plots with uplifting themes that celebrated humanity. The show was an ingrained part of the American culture for ten years and hugely popular right up to the end. The odd thing that I noticed, though, was that many people who were casual viewers of *MASH* thought that it was set in the Vietnam War, even though all the references were clearly toward the actual setting, the Korean War. I guess that is just another indication that the Korean War was truly "the forgotten war" and the Vietnam War was on people's minds.

The Vietnam War is certainly much more on the minds of my generation. The Vietnam experience will always be part of who we are, even for those of us who never actually got to Vietnam then, and we won't forget 1968, the year America was falling apart. The Viet Cong and North Vietnamese armies launched the Tet Offensive on January 30 that year. It would be the largest campaign initiated by either side during the war. It included attacks upon what had been thought to be safe American strongholds, especially the South Vietnamese capital of Saigon. The attackers were beaten back with heavy casualties on both sides. But the senselessness and ugliness of the war had again been reinforced.

As the 1968 presidential primary elections began, Senator Eugene McCarthy of Minnesota, running as an antiwar candidate, was providing a formidable challenge to President Johnson on the Democratic side.[30] A dejected LBJ got the message and announced that he would not continue to run for another term. At this point, Robert Kennedy jumped into the race. Both McCarthy and Kennedy pledged to get the US out of Vietnam. The other Democratic presidential candidate was Hubert Humphrey, who was vice-president under Johnson. Kennedy expressed interest in a wide range of social reforms and excited young people with the thought of Camelot reborn and ascending to new heights, remaking America to embrace the full meaning of liberty, justice and equality. Humphrey also proposed a program of social reforms which were to be an extension of the Great Society. Humphrey, however, could not pledge to get the US out of Vietnam because he was part of the administration conducting the war.

The American army appeared to be breaking down. The Tet offensive had just ended when it became known that an American platoon had massacred an entire village of civilians (My Lai). Strangely this event did not seem to really shock many people at home, nor did it precipitate any large scale investigation or reassessment of the Vietnam policy. Those Americans opposed to the war were already outraged; those not opposed were often numb to the news coming out of Vietnam. Such massacres were predictable because of the way the war was being conducted. No one really expected the US (and the South Vietnamese) to win, but no one at home expected the US to give up either. Soldiers were sent to Vietnam for a one year deployment with no illusions that they would make any progress in winning the war. So the goal of the American soldier became to stay alive, complete a year, and go home, with no larger noble cause. So, what does the soldier do when he encounters a village which he knows to include enemy sympathizers who might later kill him? I am not saying that the murder of civilians is justified, only that it probably happened on more than just one occasion. A captain and a lieutenant were convicted in the My Lai case. No higher ranking officers were charged, though they had

---

[30] Eugene McCarthy is not to be confused with "Jittery" Joe McCarthy, the fanatic anti-communism senator from Wisconsin of the early 1950s, from whom we got the term "McCarthyism."

to be aware of the climate under their command—higher ranking officers were either complicit or incompetent. For career NCOs and officers, the one year hitch meant get in, get out, get promoted, and don't worry about the outcomes.

Discontent with the war was sparking frequent protests and stirring growing disrespect for the law. Racial tensions added to the breakdown of law and order. The 1964 Civil Rights Act and the 1965 Voter Rights Act seemed to promise needed reforms, but they did not instantly cure the severe discrimination which was still frustrating African-Americans. Race riots had become common in the summers since 1965. The worst of these may have been the Watts, California riot in August of that year. Watts was ninety-eight percent African-American but its police force was nearly all white. The arrest of a Watts motorist for reckless driving escalated into an affair which lasted six days. Restoring order required 15,000 police and the California National Guard. When the riot was over thirty-four people had been killed and nearly 4,000 arrested, and two hundred businesses had been destroyed.[31] Richard Nixon, who had lost his bid for president in 1960, then lost the governor's race in California in 1962 and famously declared to the press that "You won't have Nixon to kick around anymore," came back from the dead to seize the Republican presidential nomination, pledging to restore law and order, end the Vietnam War, and stop the inflation. (Inflation fueled by government deficit spending was running high and threatening to destroy the prosperity of the 1960s.)

With political passions feverish in 1968 among Americans of all persuasions, the two most iconic and charismatic leaders for social justice and against the Vietnam War at that time were assassinated within weeks of each other. Martin Luther King was cut down by a sniper at a Memphis hotel that April. This led to widespread rioting. Then in June, Robert Kennedy was shot at pointblank range at a hotel in Los Angeles just minutes after completing his victory speech on winning the California Democratic Primary. Racially fueled riots continued in major cities all that summer while many young people were becoming more and more alienated from society and angry with the government. In the long run, Martin King's martyrdom seems to have galvanized the cause of civil rights as white people came to revere and cherish the values he represented, but the loss of Robert Kennedy seems only to have further alienated

---

[31] Rubel, David, *Scholastic Encyclopedia of the Presidents and Their Times* (New York: Scholastic, Inc., 1994) page 177.

the youth of his day by extinguishing what many saw as the last great hope for America.

As the primary election season was coming to a close, Hubert Humphrey had the lead in delegates on the Democratic side and appeared certain to gain the nomination. Humphrey was a decent man who wanted to do good things for the country and had waited faithfully in line for his turn to be president, but what he did not seem to realize was that regardless of his intentions his candidacy was not good the for the country at that time. If he had had greater vision or more genuine concern for the country, he might have stepped aside.[32] A large number of war protesters flooded into Chicago from all over the country for the Democratic National Convention. Trouble seemed to be certain, and Chicago Major Richard Daily ordered the police out in a heavy show of force. Violent confrontation between the police and the protesters occurred with many protesters injured and many arrested. Eight of the protest leaders, "the Chicago 8", were charged with a felony crime of crossing state lines to incite a riot. The trial of the African-American protest leader, Bobby Seale, became big news. Seale, a co-founder of the Black Panthers, would not be silent and disrupted proceedings so much that the judge ordered him bound and gagged during much of his trial. Months after the Convention, a detailed government investigation found that much of the fault in Chicago that summer was hostility and overreaction on the part of the police, calling the affair "a police riot."[33] Such was the condition of America in 1968.

I was in the army at the time. I confess that I would have voted for Richard Nixon if I had been old enough to vote, expecting him to stop the war. But during the campaign he didn't actually say outright that he would stop the war. What he said was "I have a plan" to end US involvement in Vietnam. He refused to divulge that plan during the campaign, but made it known upon his election. His plan was "Vietnamization," gradually reducing American

---

[32] However, with Robert Kennedy now dead, there was no other strong candidate among the Democratic aspirants.

[33] Daniel Walker, "Rights in Conflict: The violent confrontation of demonstrators and police in the parks and streets of Chicago during the week of the Democratic National Convention of 1968," a report submitted by the Chicago Study Team, to the National Commission on the Causes and Prevention of Violence, December 1, 1968.

troop strength in Vietnam while training recruits to the South Vietnamese army. Nixon's plan would cost thousands of American lives and have no positive effect. Nixon had already earned the moniker "Tricky Dick" well before this latest, cruelest trick.

Nixon won the presidency in 1968 decisively in the electoral college, but the popular vote was actually very close. The entry of a third party candidate, who did astonishingly well, probably took more votes from Nixon than from Humphrey. Former Alabama Governor George Wallace, who had once declared "segregation now segregation forever", captured five southern states.

The war dragged on four more years and beyond. The number of US troops in Vietnam was reduced significantly in that time and the size of the South Vietnamese army did increase. But the outcome seemed never to have been in doubt. The government of South Vietnam, which was totally undemocratic, appeared to have little popular support outside Saigon and Da Nang, so Vietnamization would only delay the inevitable, causing greater misery, while allowing the US the appearance of an honorable exit. As many young people saw it, the President's Vietnam policy benefited only the President. Thousands more Americans would die, many more would be seriously wounded, and countless Vietnamese would die, all to further the career of Richard Nixon. I saw the President as a man without honor. While a sudden pullout would have been a betrayal of a significant number of Vietnamese who were in support of the US, a negotiated capitulation with protection guarantees for US supporters would have been an honorable solution.

Nixon's dilemma was that the US had never lost a war. A US defeat would have tanked Nixon's career and threatened his historical legacy, so a few thousand more American deaths were acceptable to him and Vietnamese lives seem never to even have been considered. No one should have to die to save face for America or get Richard Nixon reelected. LBJ had overseen the massive build-up of American forces in Vietnam, because he was naive, and his view of the world was limited, but Richard Nixon knew full-well what he was doing. I can try to understand Johnson's actions. Jesus said, "Father, forgive them; they know not what they do." However, I cannot condone the actions of Richard Nixon. I think he knew what he was doing.

Protests grew larger and more frequent during President Nixon's first term. The news from Vietnam grew more appalling. The massacre of the Vietnamese village of My Lai had been reported in March 1968 and the army prosecuted only the captain and lieutenant in charge—no one else—as if this was an isolated incident. Agent Orange was used as a "defoliant", as if a chemical agent could miraculously kill plants without harming animal or human life. When the war was extended into Cambodia in the spring of 1970, protesters at Kent State University in Ohio were met by National Guard troops who became unnerved and fired on the protesters, killing four.

Nixon became more hated than LBJ had been, despite actually scoring some Cold War breakthroughs. He negotiated two treaties with the Soviets to reduce the threat of nuclear war, and he was able to establish détente, a state of peaceful coexistence with the Soviet Union. He also became the first American president to visit Communist China, the first step to the subsequent normalization of US-China relations. This was especially noteworthy because he had built his early career as a kind of disciple of Jittery Joe McCarthy chasing communists in the State Department.

Major Cultural and World Events of the 1960s

1960	Hawaii becomes the fiftieth state.	
1961	Adolf Eichmann, Israelis most wanted former Nazi, is abducted from his Argentine refuge, brought to trial, and condemned to death in Israel.	
1962	Rachel Carson publishes *Silent Spring*.	Carson made a strong case against the use of pesticides and a grim warning about humans poisoning the planet. This is the first great environmentalist book.
1963	Betty Friedan publishes *The Feminine Mystique*.	*The Feminine Mystique* is a benchmark book in the history of the Women's Liberation Movement. It challenges women to find their own place in society.
1963	The Beatles have their first number 1 hit in the UK, "She Loves You."[34]	"She loves you—yah, yah, yah." "And with a love like that you know you should be glad."
1965	Ralph Nader publishes *Unsafe at Any Speed*, an indictment of the American auto industry's lack of attention to safety issues.	One result of this book is that regulations are imposed on the auto industry to install seatbelts in all cars. A larger result is that Nader has begun a national movement of consumer advocacy which he will continue to lead.

---

[34] "Beatlemania," Phelps and Courtenay-Thompson, managing editors, p.232.

1966	The National Organization of Women (NOW) is formed with Betty Freidan as one of the founding members.	

1966	The Supreme Court under Earl Warren issues the verdict in Miranda v. Arizona.	This is the Court decision which specified rights of the accused, the best known of which is that suspects must be informed of their rights and provided with an attorney before interrogation.
1967	South African physician, Christiaan Barnard, performs the world's first human heart transplant.	
1967	In its Six Day War with Arab neighbors, Israel emerges victorious with territorial gains in the West Bank of the Jordan River, the Sinai Peninsula, and the Golan Heights.	By International law established in 1945, lands taken in war must be returned. Israel has not yet returned the West Bank or the Golan Heights.
1969	Neil Armstrong became the first man to walk on the moon July 21, 1969.	
1969	"Stonewall riots" in New York City occur as gay and lesbians fight back against police harassment.	This was the result of frequent raids by police on The Stonewall Bar in Greenwich Village, New York. These riots are considered to be the beginning of the gay rights movement.
1969	*Sesame Street* premiers.	*Sesame Street* continued on public television for almost 50 years, teaching children letters, numbers, and kindness.

4

The 1970s

The Music of Our Lives

The youth counter-culture which evolved in the 1960s and 70s was a sane reaction to insane America. The Woodstock Music Festival in 1969 is the great symbol of that counter-culture. I may be in the minority by admitting that I did not attend, nor was I even aware of the event until after. But it was a great shining achievement for my generation. The promoters had planned for 200,000 paid attendees, but over 400,000 showed up and broke down the fences. The promoters had to have been desperate. They would likely lose money, and they might also be sued if the event turned into an ugly riot. To avoid this, they frequently reminded the attendees that this was a chance to prove to the world that America did not have to be the ugly nation of Richard Nixon, that a better America could be built. It worked. Rains came and made conditions harsher, but concert-goers remained for the most part calm and highly civilized. A minor miracle had occurred. The Woodstock site had been officially designated as a "disaster area."[35]

Music was an intricate part of the counter-culture, and to my mind music, had never been better, and it has not been as good since. Four high quality concert programs competed for the late night television audience on Fridays and Saturdays in the early 1970s. These were *In Concert, Don Kershner's Rock Concert, The Midnight Special* with Wolfman Jack, and *Austin City Limits*. Many of the songs of the 60s and 70s were topical. Years later, as a history teacher, I was able to build lessons chronicling this period around some of the iconic songs. "The Times" were "A-Changin'" rapidly. My counter-culture lessons began with this and "For What it's Worth", as Bob Dylan and Buffalo Springfield proclaimed a new era. According to Dylan

---

[35] For anyone who is interested, there was an excellent documentary film made about *Woodstock*.

> The old world is rapidly fadin'
> So get out of the new one if you can't lend a hand
> For the times they are a changin'[36]

The Buffalo Springfield song, "For What It's Worth", also presaged things to come with:

> Somethin' happenin' here.
> What it is ain't exactly clear.
> There's a man with a gun over there
> Tell me I got to beware.
> You better stop children
> What's that song?
> Everybody look what's going on.[37]

Another widely popular song of the time which could also be included in this lesson is "(Nothing Can Change) The Shape of Things to Come" by Max Frost and the Troopers. Among the most iconic songs of the time is the hilarious rant against the draft, "Alice's Restaurant", which was written and performed by Arlo Guthrie.[38] It's the story of a young man who reported for his draft physical and was deferred from military service for having been a "litter bug." You really have to hear the whole 18 minutes to fully appreciate it. I recently attended an Arlo Guthrie concert and was surprised and delighted to hear him still performing "Alice's Restaurant" in its entirety nearly, fifty years later. The rest of the audience also appeared to be equally delighted.

Some popular songs written in the late 60s and early 70s chronicled specific events. Graham Nash wanted Americans to know about the trial of Bobby Seale with an upbeat message in "Chicago—We Can Change the World"

> **Though your brother's bound and gagged**
> **And they've chained him to a chair**
> **Won't you please come to Chicago just to sing?**
> **In a land that's known as freedom**
> **How can such a thing be fair?**

---

[36] Dylan, Bob, "The Times they are A-Changin'": 1965.

[37] Stills, Stephen, Buffalo Springfield, "For What It's Worth": 1967

[38] Arlo Guthrie, "Aice's Restaurant" on *Alice's Restaurant, Warner Bros. Records,* 1967.

Won't you please come to Chicago
For the help that you can bring?[39]

The point that this trial was highly irregular and smelled of injustice is well made, but I should also point out that Bobby Seale might not be considered a heroic figure.

Woodstock featured Country Joe McDonald singing the "I-Feel-Like-I'm-Fixin'-to-Die Rag"

> Well come on all you big strong men
> Uncle Sam needs your help again
> Got himself in a terrible jam
> Way down yonder in Vietnam
> So put down your books and pick up a gun
> We're gonna have a whole lot of fun.
> And its 1-2-3-What are we fighting for?[40]

Joni Mitchell, who was not actually at Woodstock, nonetheless wrote a song about the Woodstock experience which she recorded, but it was actually made famous by Crosby, Stills, Nash, and Young, who, except for Neil Young, were there:

> By the time we got to Woodstock
> We were half a million strong
> And everywhere was a song and celebration.
> We are stars
> We all know just who we are
> And we got to get ourselves back to the garden.[41]

The 1970 Kent State Massacre of four university students by panicked Ohio National Guard during the protest of the US invasion of Cambodia was the subject of "Ohio", also by Crosby, Stills, Nash, and Young. They suggest in this song a call to action.

> Tin soldiers and Nixon's comin'

---

[39] Nash, Graham, "Chicago—We Can Change the World" contained in *Songs for Beginners*, 1968.

[40] McDonald, Country Joe and the Fish, "I Feel-Like- I'm-Fixin-to-Die Rag:" 1969

[41] Mitchell, Joni, "Woodstock" performed by Crosby, Stills, Nash, and Young: 1969.

We're finally on our own.
This summer I hear the drummin'
Four dead in O-hi-o
Gotta' get down to it.
Soldiers are cutting us down.
Should have been done long ago.
What if you knew her and found her dead on the ground?...[42]

For anyone interested in more songs about Vietnam or the Vietnam experience, I would point to the works of Pete Seeger, Tom Paxton, and Phil Ochs. Seeger and the Smothers Brothers met with opposition from CBS when the brothers decided to have the previously "black listed" folk artist preform "Waste Deep in the Big Muddy" on *The Smothers Brothers Comedy Hour.* The song was cut from the show, and the Brothers protested to the network. After some haggling, the network relented, and Seeger was allowed to perform the song in a later episode.[43] "Silent Night—Seven O'clock News" by Simon and Garfunkel also captured the essence of this time period. I liked to finish my Vietnam era lesson with "Sam Stone" by John Prine.

Sam Stone
Came home
To his wife and family
After serving in the conflict overseas
And the time that he served
Had shattered all his nerves
And left a little shrapnel in his knee.[44]

The themes are emotional scars and suicide. The story of Sam Stone does not end well. Prine also wrote a song which has become a kind of counter-culture anthem which I could not play for my high school students, *Illegal Smile.*

You may see me tonight with an illegal smile.
It don't cost very much

---

[42] Young, Neil, "Ohio" performed by Crosby, Stills, Nash, and Young: 1970

[43] Turnquist, Kristi, "Pete Seeger and the Smothers Brothers censorship fight: TV Talk," *The Oregonian, Oregon Live*: January 28, 2014.

[44] Prine, John, "Sam Stone": 1974.

> But it lasts a long while.
> Won't you please tell the man
> I didn't kill anyone?
> I'm just tryin' to have me some fun.[45]

As the reader can plainly see, music is a big part of who I am, even though I have no musical talent. My obsession with the music of the 60s and 70s is undying. This is characteristic of many boomers. That is why so much of the music of this period is still all around us today.

In my opinion, the last good music was that of The Eagles, Bruce Springsteen, and Jimmy Buffet. The Eagles *Greatest Hits* album recently surpassed Michael's Jackson's *Thriller* to become the top selling album of all times. Springsteen's *Born in the* USA is also among the top selling albums of all time. And Buffet's *Livin' and Dyin' in Three Quarter Time* is one of my absolute favorite albums. I'm still a parrot head, and disco sucks! As the 70s turned to the 80s new popular music just didn't interest me much. My tastes turned to country—but not mainstream country; country with an edge and some sophistication. I listened to Jerry Jeff Walker, Waylon Jennings, Willie Nelson, David Alan Coe, Emmylou Harris, the soulful sound of Patsy Cline; and I continued to listen to Linda Ronstadt, a Tucson girl, who always had that southwest, Latina country edge with pop crossover appeal. Her music became more sophisticated in the 70s. During that time she produced two exceptional albums, *Hasten Down the Wind* (1976) and *Prisoner in Disguise* (1975). But her earliest work with the Stone Poneys is also impressive. "Different Drum" is a classic.

More recently I discovered the Bellamy Brothers who spoke directly to their fellow boomers with "Kids of the Baby Boom" and "Old Hippie." "Kids of the Baby Boom" encapsulates many of the most common boomer experiences. This is how it starts

> Our daddy's won the war and came home to our moms
> They gave them so much love that all us kids were born
> We all grew up on Mickey Mouse and hula-hoops
> Then we all bought BMW's and brand new pickup trucks
> And we watched John Kennedy die one afternoon
> Kids of the baby boom

---

[45] Prine, John, "Illegal Smile": 1975.

It was a time of new prosperity in the USA
All the fortunate offspring never had to pay...[46]

"Old Hippie" is more specifically about my lost generation:

He's an old hippie
And he don't know what to do
Should he hold on to the old?
Should he grab on to the new?
He's an old hippie
He ain't tryin' to make a fuss.
He's just trying real hard
To adjust.[47]

I felt for a long time that I was caught in a time warp. The world was changing and it didn't make sense. In some ways, many of us boomers are still in the 1960s-70s time warp and always will be.

A Shady Dealer and a Used Ford

I was old enough to vote in a presidential election for the first time in 1972. George McGovern was the Democratic candidate running against Nixon. McGovern based his entire campaign on stopping the Vietnam War, refusing to discuss other issues on anything but a superficial level. Then about two weeks before the election President Nixon announce that an agreement had been reached and all American combat troops would be withdrawn from Vietnam soon. This pronouncement proved to be premature and deceptive, but effective—"Tricky Dick" in action.[48] McGovern lost badly. Nixon won 49 states. McGovern won only in Massachusetts and the District of Columbia. I'm proud to say I voted for George McGovern. Before the campaign was over some burglars were caught at the headquarters of the Democratic Party in the Watergate Hotel

---

[46] Bellamy Brothers, "Kids of the Baby Boom": 1987.

[47] Bellamy Brothers, "Old Hippie": 1985.

[48] Henry Kissinger and his North Vietnamese counterpart Le Duc Tho received the 1973 Nobel Peace for the peace agreement, but armed military conflict continued between North and South Vietnam with the US acting mainly in a support role until the communist victory in 1975.

in Washington, D.C. They were sent there by CREEP, the Committee to Reelect the President. (I did not make up the acronym. It was their own.) This began the infamous Watergate scandal (and the reason why future political scandals would all be labeled "... gate").

As we came to find out later, the President was immediately informed of the situation and tried to cover it up. A congressional investigation dragged on into the summer of 1974. Nixon was discovered to have been making tapes of Oval Office conversations and Congress eventually force him to turn over these tapes, one of which had a mysteriously large gap which had been mistakenly (conveniently) erased. Transcripts of some of the tapes were released to the press. I was not particularly shocked by the content, except that the language Nixon and his team were using sounded like a group of sixth grade boys talking dirty on the playground. Nixon was caught, but he was not one to go down without first trying to throw someone else down in his place. Vice-president Spiro Agnew soon found himself being investigated for wrong doing when he was governor of Maryland. He was forced from office and convicted, while the Watergate investigation continued and Nixon's impeachment proceedings began.

With the vice-presidency vacant, Nixon was able to appoint a vice-president of his own choosing, though subject to the approval of the Senate. He chose Congressman Gerald Ford even as the Watergate Investigation went forward. The House of Representatives voted to move the impeachment forward to trial in the Senate, at which time Nixon became the only president to ever resign, and Gerald Ford became the only US president who was never elected as either president or vice-president. This strange comic affair was concluded when Ford, in his first official act as president, issued a pardon of Richard Nixon for "any crimes which he may have committed while in office." Who would have thought that anyone could be pardoned of unspecified crimes without first being convicted or even indicted? Only in Nixon World. If I took a cynical view, I might be tempted to say that America had been sold a used Ford by a shady dealer, but I don't really believe that that was the case. I believe that President Ford sincerely wanted to help America put the Watergate Affair in the past and move forward. He was a decent man.

The entertainment of the day reflected the absurdity of Nixon World. Mel Brooks gave us *Blazing Saddles*, one of my favorite movies. He followed it with *Young Frankenstein*, which is equally funny. Cheech and Chong were making wild comedy albums. They also made a couple funny movies and had a following, before they started making disgusting movies which insulted and alienated their fans. *The Exorcist* also appeared in 1973, a truly scary horror movie. I don't believe in any of this, but this film was so frightening that I had to survey the back seat of my car very carefully before I got in it to drive home the night I saw it.

I got married for the first time in 1972 and I soon had a son. Putting my university studies on hold, I worked in factory as a machine operator for two years. Then my restless nature had my little family move out west to Colorado. The whole country was moving west. I was too immature and too selfish to be a good husband or a good father, and I was soon confronted with divorce, which was more traumatic for me then than it would be today. People still did not commonly get divorced then. I was the first in my social circle, so I (rightly) blamed myself and nearly had a nervous breakdown. I took well over a year to fully recover. But life goes on. I can laugh about my pathetic state now, but I wasn't laughing then.

I got my sense of humor back watching Woody Allen movies. *Play it Again Sam* allowed me to laugh at myself. In it Allen is a man depressed from being dumped by his wife and obsessed with the classic movie *Casablanca*, fantasizing about being Rick the movie's hero.[49] I like all the older Woody Allen movies. *Sleeper* is among my favorites. Woody Allen does his best slapstick in it. All the Woody Allen movies have this wonderful, uplifting, self-effacing humor which does not victimize anyone and is all too rare in our society. Allen was at the top of his game in the 70s, making exceptional movies which are timeless. The two Woody Allen movies which are really top quality are *Annie Hall* (1977), which won Allen Oscars for best director and best screenplay, and *Manhattan* (1979), which many critics say is even better than *Annie Hall*; I agree. *Manhattan* is great cinematic art. Black-and-white photography is used deliberately and carefully and set to a well-selected soundtrack of Gershwin music.

---

[49] *Casablanca* is my all-time favorite movie.

A New America Rising

Gerald Ford was a well-meaning president but maybe not quite up to the job. He oversaw the panicked evacuation of Americans from Vietnam in 1975. His solution for the inflation problem was to commission lapel buttons with the slogan WIN, Whip Inflation Now. It didn't help. To his credit, he didn't create any new problems and he brought a much needed calmness to the country. He was even, in a way, inspirational. He inspired Chevy Chase. The new experimental *Saturday Night Live* premiered in 1975. Chase would open the show with a skit in which he portrayed President Ford and ended up falling down. Sketch comedy was not entirely new. *Rowan and Martin's Laugh- In* had run successfully from 1968 to 1973 and made Goldie Hawn a star. But *Laugh-In* aired in primetime and appealed to mainstream America. *Saturday Night Live,* in contrast, occupied the 10:30PM slot on Saturday night, the near perfect day and time for an experimental program since no one was watching anyway, and it was aimed at young adults. The original *Saturday Night Live* was really innovative and special. The cast, "The Not Quite Ready for Prime Time Players," was more than ready; they were exceptionally talented—Chevy Chase, Dan Aykroyd, Garrett Morris, John Belushi, Gilda Radner, Jane Curtin, and Laraine Newman. The show also had interesting guest hosts who were not always superstars—Buck Henry was one. And they had interesting musical guests who often were just becoming popular. Al Franken, later Senator Al Franken, was one of the writers and made occasional bit appearances.[50] After only one year Chevy Chase left to become a movie star. He was replaced by Bill Murray and the show got even better, as it became less dependent on any one cast member. The magic lasted for all of the first three seasons, but began to fade by the fourth season. Steven Martin became a frequent guest host during the last two years in which the original cast was featured. He had appeared often on *The Tonight Show* (with Johnny Carson), but his appearances on *SNL* were what made him a star.

As a cultural phenomenon, *Saturday Night Live* influenced millions of lifestyles on those first five years. Back then no one had a video recorder. So, if you didn't watch the show when it was scheduled, you missed it completely. What I did, and saw many

---

[50] Franken had established himself as intelligent, forceful voice in the Democratic Party before being caught up in the sex scandals of 2017 and forced from office.

other 20 somethings doing, was to go out to the bars on Saturday night to listen to a band until almost 10:30.[51] Then we all hurried home to catch *Saturday Night Live* from the beginning. No one would do this for the recent incarnations of the show. They aren't at all special.

As a matter of fact, *SNL* was almost cancelled because the quality deteriorated so much in the sixth season after the entire original cast left. The show was saved by nineteen-year-old Eddy Murphy. For a while *SNL* really became "the Eddy Murphy show." Then another generation of fairly talented artists took charge, and the show became entertaining again, if not spectacular, in the 1980s. Al Franken continued with the show and was more frequently in front of the camera. This is when *SNL* became an established institution which would not die despite being frequently mediocre.

Television was really maturing in the late 1970s. *SNL* is only one example of this. The other amazing innovation was the mini-series—a serious, important story told over 10 to 20 hours, often shown over several consecutive nights. The first two miniseries set a standard which have never been equaled. The first was *Holocaust*. The topic of the Holocaust was effectively humanized with a story of fictional characters caught up in it. The fictional format allowed the writers to tell a complex story of the entire German society of the time—Nazis, anti-Nazis, common folk caught up in history, soldiers, and Jews in various circumstances. *Holocaust* was a huge success and showed how television could be used to educate a mass audience and still be entertaining, popular, and profitable. The next even bigger miniseries was *Roots*, the story of an African-American family from the abduction of the patriarch as a young man in Africa to the liberation of the family generations later at the end of the Civil War. *Roots* was not fictional in the same mode as *Holocaust,* but was based on research done by the author, Alex Haley, about his own ancestors. The educational value of *Holocaust* and *Roots* cannot be overestimated. These programs touched people deeply, educating emotions and attitudes. Both were so good and so successful that it is surprising that after this start the miniseries never achieved anything close to this quality again.

1976 was the bicentennial year. It was also a presidential

---

[51] Yes, many bars had a live band on weekends. The cover charge was a dollar or two, and the bands were excellent.

election year. Former California Governor Ronald Reagan challenged incumbent President Ford for the Republican nomination and almost succeeded. Reagan won several primaries including the big state races of Texas and California. In the final count of delegates at the Republican National Convention, Reagan had 1,070, just a little short of the 1,129 needed for victory. Jimmy Carter, a peanut farmer and one term governor of Georgia, who also happened to be a US Naval Academy graduate and a nuclear engineer, defeated President Ford in the general election with the simple promise, "I will never lie to you." President Ford certainly was not a liar, but he was tainted by having been associated with Richard Nixon. The importance placed on truth in that campaign is emblematic of just how low our standards had been driven by Nixon's presidency. Except perhaps on rare occasions, when compelled for reasons of national security, we had come to expect our president to tell the truth, until Nixon broke that trust.

Carter was, and still is, a good and decent man, but a bit of a preacher. That was his biggest flaw as president. He could not work with Congress because he did not care to compromise. He developed solutions and presented them to Congress on a take it or leave it basis. When Congress balked, Carter tried to plea directly to the American people with televised "fireside chats". But he wasn't FDR, and perhaps fireside chats played better on the radio. These efforts came across as staged and silly. The inflation, which had plagued the Nixon and Ford administrations, remained high and increased to 9% in 1979 and nearly 14% in 1980, causing a dismal downturn in the economy.

With his domestic efforts thwarted, Carter turned to international affairs and performed a minor miracle. He brokered a peace agreement between Israel and Egypt (the Camp David Accords). Because Egypt is the largest and militarily strongest of the Arab nations, this agreement had the effect of guaranteeing that there would be no more major Arab-Israeli wars.[52] Of course there is still a real Arab-Israeli Conflict. And former President Carter has worked hard for many years now to help solve this conflict also.

Despite the Camp David achievement, Carter's presidency seemed fated to fail. His foreign policy suffered a major setback when the Shaw of Iran came to the US for cancer treatment.

---

[52] Militant Arabs and militant Israelis were displeased with the Accords. Egyptian President Anwar Sadat was assassinated for signing it.

While the Shaw was here, a revolution overthrew his government. Revolutionaries stormed the American Embassy in Tehran and took 50 Americans, who were in the Embassy at that time, hostage. The new Iranian government demanded return of the Shaw in exchange for the American hostages. This certainly could not be done. The Shaw had been a ruthless dictator, but also a loyal American ally. And the American CIA had been influential in putting him in power in the first place. The Shaw was eventually allowed sanctuary in Panama for the remaining few months of his life, but the hostage crisis continued. A failed rescue attempt saw an American helicopter crash with fatalities in a desert sand storm. The hostage crisis dogged President Carter as he campaigned for reelection against Ronald Reagan in 1980.

The Carter administration took the high road in its relationship with Latin-America, refusing to give the CIA free reign to covertly manipulate governments, as had been the standard Cold War policy. Communist leadership had always been stymied by CIA opposition. Now the lid was off and Central America erupted. In 1979 a communist government came to power in Nicaragua, a communist revolution was begun in El Salvador, and a long-running insurgency continued in Guatemala. American conservatives blamed Carter, but the causes were right-wing, dictatorial governments in these countries. Carter was right in reversing policies of interference, but short-run results alarmed Americans.

Major Cultural and World Events of the 1970s

1970	Germaine Greer publishes *The Feminine Eunuch.*[53]	*The Feminine Eunuch* is a benchmark book in the Women's Liberation Movement.
1970	Jordan's King Hussein expels radical Palestinians from the kingdom after a brief civil war, which became known as "Black September."	
1972	Terrorists from the Palestinian Black September Group break into the Israeli Olympic team residence, killing two and taking nine hostages. The hostages and their captors are all killed in a later shoot out.	
1972	Mark Spitz wins a record 7 Gold Medals in swimming events during the 1972 Olympics.	Spitz's extraordinary record is expected to last indefinitely, but it is broken by Michael Phelps in 2008.
1973	In the Case of Roe v. Wade the Supreme Court rules 7-2 that states cannot prohibit a woman from having an abortion before the "fetal viability" stage of pregnancy.	

---

[53] Phelps and Courtenay-Thompson, managing editors, "Germaine Greer introduces The Feminine Eunuch," p. 259.

1975	The first personal home computers come on the market.[54]	
1975	October 11, *Saturday Night Live* debuts with guest host George Carlin.	
1976	*The Rocky Horror Picture Show* is released.	This becomes a cult classic and the midnight movie on Saturday night at many theaters for years to come.
1979	The US suffers its only nuclear plant accident.	A near meltdown occurred at the Three Mile Island nuclear plant near Harrisburg, Pennsylvania.

---

[54] Ibid. "Computers Get Personal," p. 274

5

The 1980s and the Regan Revolution

Ronald Reagan, was elected president in 1980, and he revived all the Cold War rhetoric, which progressives had hoped was behind us. I saw America moving backward to a darker time. To conservatives, the new president offered a feeling of hope for "morning in America," renewal and revitalization. On the day of President Reagan's inauguration, the American hostages were released from Iran after 444 days of captivity. Wonderful! But the Reagan administration went on to develop a suspiciously cozy relationship with Iran. As president, Reagan had charm and luck going for him. Two months after taking office he was shot by a would-be assassin—a crazy man with no political agenda. The bullet was close to the President's heart, but he recovered. I was as happy as everyone else about his recovery. I didn't agree with much of what Reagan wanted to do, but I certainly didn't want him to die. Interestingly, Reagan would go on to be America's oldest president, and he would also break the infamous "20 year curse." Presidents elected every 20 years beginning in 1840 had died in office.[55]

President Reagan deserves credit for resetting the American economy in 1981. Previous presidents had been reluctant to allow a recession for political reasons, but a recession was what was needed to put a stop to the inflationary pressure which was inhibiting real economic growth. Reagan's "supply-side economics" required cutting government spending and cutting taxes. The country went into a deep but brief recession in 1981-82 then bounced back healthier than ever. Supply-side ("trickle down") economics worked, but Reagan did not stay with it because he had a Cold War agenda.

---

[55] William H. Harrison, 1840, caught pneumonia on his inauguration day and died a month later; Abraham Lincoln, 1860, was assassinated; James Garfield, 1880, was assassinated; William McKinley, 1900, was assassinated; Warren G. Harding, 1920, died of a heart attack in1923; Franklin Roosevelt, 1940, died of a stroke in April 1945, a month before VE Day; John Kennedy, 1960, was assassinated.

He greatly increased government spending for the military. This led to large increases in the national debt with which our government is still coping today.

I believe President Reagan's Cold War policies toward Nicaragua and El Salvador may have been well-meaning in an arrogant, paternalistic way, but they were backward and presumptive. No country has the right to dictate to another what type of government it should have. That idea was wrong in the 1950s and 60s when the CIA was doing it as a component of Cold War strategy, and the long-run effects of US manipulation then proved to have been counterproductive in Iran and much of Latin America, and nowhere more so than in Nicaragua, where US interference predated the CIA. US Marines had exerted American control in that country for 20 years from 1912 to 1933. When these troops finally left, the US was influential in installing the Somoza family as dictatorial rulers.

By 1981 even the appearance of Cold War necessity was lifted. Neither Nicaragua nor El Salvador were in any remote way a threat to the United States. Democratic capitalism had proven to be vastly superior to autocratic socialism. The domino theory no longer applied, if it ever did. At the time Ronald Reagan entered the presidency, Nicaragua had experienced the recent communist revolution which deposed the last Somoza dictator. The country was stable with no apparent anti-communist insurgency. Reagan went about trying to create a revolution where none existed. He recruited an army of mercenaries, the Contras, which existed only because the Contra soldiers were paid by the United States. In El Salvador, on the other hand, Reagan did find a revolution. Communists there were attempting to overthrow a brutal dictatorship. The US, under Reagan, supported the dictator. In one infamous incident, four Catholic nuns were raped and murdered by government soldiers. When this was discovered, Reagan's Secretary of State, Alexander Haig, in an affront to decency, suggested that the nuns may have run a roadblock.[56]

Eventually the situation in El Salvador settled down with some US insistence on reform. Nicaragua would also have settled down without the flow of US dollars to the Contras. The US Congress finally passed a bill demanding that no more US funds could be sent to the Contras. This should have been the end, except for a diabolical, determined lieutenant colonel, Oliver North, working

---

[56]   www.upi.com/Archives/1981/03/18/Secretary-of-State-Alexander-Haig-told-a-congressional-hearing/3791353739600/

in the basement of the White House. He wanted to sell military equipment to Iran—also contrary to Congressional restrictions. The equipment was sold, then the funds were funneled to the Contras. Thus no money was reported to have been exchanged regarding these two illegal activities. When the scheme was discovered, President Reagan's only defense was that he was unaware of these transactions. Any other president would have been impeached, but Reagan, the Teflon President, was popular and nearing the end of his second term by the time the affair was fully investigated.[57]

Reagan is also often credited with winning the Cold War by forcing the Soviets to increase military spending, while negotiating a nuclear arms reduction treaty with them. He deserves credit for the treaty, but the loosening of Soviet control of satellite countries and the eventual break-up of the Soviet Union probably had less to do with US pressure than with long-term internal factors within the Soviet Union. The problem the Soviet Union had was that Joseph Stalin had so thoroughly purged the Soviet Communist Party that what remained was an extremely tight core of survivors with much the same mindset, all working together to maintain power. As the years past they got older and died off. Mikhail Gorbachev, who came to power as the Communist Party General Secretary in 1985, was the first of the next generation of Soviet leaders. He saw how the Soviet Union had fallen behind the west and was failing its own people, and he came with the will to make some long overdue changes. He advocated "glasnost" (new openness—free speech which would allow Soviet citizens to criticize the government) and "perestroika" (restructuring--of the economy to include elements of capitalism).

The pace of change which resulted from glasnost and perestroika was almost miraculous, and it soon overwhelmed everyone, not the least Gorbachev himself. First, the Soviet Union began to lose control of its eastern bloc of satellite countries. Then the Soviet Union itself imploded. The fifteen republics of the Soviet Union essentially had represented fifteen ethnicities with the Russian Republic, larger than the other fourteen combined, dominating. Many of the other republics were found to be unhappy with this arrangement. Once

---

[57] Reagan had also escaped any serious repercussions when 239 US Marines died in Beirut, victims of a bomb. Reagan accepted responsibility and withdrew all US forces from Lebanon with no clear explanation as to why they were there in the first place or who was responsible for the bombing.

secession began, all the republics were independent within a few years. The Soviet Union was officially dissolved at the end of 1991. No one could have imagined the sudden, relatively peaceful end of the Soviet Union. Nor could anyone have imagined the reunification of Germany around the same time. We all rejoiced in 1989 when the Berlin Wall came down. The collapse of Communist Eastern Europe and the Soviet Union happened so rapidly, it stunned everyone. Reagan was not the cause, but his reputation benefited.

I don't think that Ronald Reagan was a particularly great president, but he wasn't bad. By today's standards he was pretty good. As expensive as his Strategic Defense Initiative was, it might still prove to have been a wise investment if it eventually provides an impenetrable shield in the face of such adversaries as North Korea. The conventional American military was also quietly reformed and modernized under Reagan. And President Reagan was able to work with a Democratic Congress, developing a good relationship with fellow Irishman and Speaker of the House, Democrat Thomas "Tip" O'Neill.

Reagan is certainly a hero to Republicans. He remade the political map. "The solid Democratic South" had shown tension and frailty for years. The southern conservative Democrats did not fit comfortably with northern progressives. The differences had clearly surfaced as early as 1948 when "Dixiecrats" bolted the Democratic Party and nominated their own presidential candidate, Strom Thurmond. John Kennedy chose Lyndon Johnson as a running mate in 1960 to hold on to the south. Kennedy's strategy did hold the Democratic coalition together that year, but in the 1964 landslide election wherein Johnson won 44 states, five of the six states he lost were in the old (former Confederate) south. By 1980 the south was ripe for a Republican takeover and Americans all over the country were weary of the reflective self-doubt, which the Vietnam War and the Nixon presidency had engendered and President Carter had embraced. Americans wanted to feel good about their country again. Ronald Reagan made people feel good about their country and themselves. He won a landslide victory over incumbent president, Jimmy Carter, winning 45 states including all of the south except Carter's home state of Georgia. When Reagan was reelected in 1984, he won 48 states, including all of the south. Since then, Democrats continue to have difficulty in the south while also losing ground among patriotic, working class people in the Midwest. Reagan captured the American flag for the Republicans, and Democrats have not yet discovered a way to get their share of it back.

The new advancement in television in the 1980s was cable TV and, with it, MTV. I think that MTV did for cable what *Bonanza* had done for color TV. People wanted cable so that they could get MTV. Every new song had to have a video, and the videos sold the records. Madonna became a big star, not because she was a great writer or a great singer, but because she was a performer. Michael Jackson became "the king of pop" with slick dance moves and his "moon walk." *Thriller* remained the top selling album of all times until the Eagles *Greatest Hits* overtook it in August 2018.

In later years Jackson was accused of child sexual abuse, first in 1993 in a case settled out of court. Another case went to trial in 2005 and Jackson was found not guilty. Jackson was known to have regularly entertained young boys overnight at his Neverland Ranch. One has to question the motives of the parents for allowing their children to sleep over in the home of a grown man. I have never been a Michael Jackson fan. I just don't care for his music, but his lifestyle was his own business. I really doubt that he ever hurt anyone in anyway.

As we moved into the 1980s, I perceived the world as changing and becoming unrecognizable for a child of the 60s. Marijuana use, which had been almost out in the open in the 60s and 70s, was more underground now, and law enforcement was more serious about it. That didn't bother me, but New Coke made me angry. Coca-Cola had been taking a beating in blind taste tests against Pepsi for some time. In 1985 the Coca-Cola Company developed a new formula to compete with Pepsi. Coke, which I and millions of others loved, was replaced with this new formula. The result was a massive boycott of the new Coke product. I think most people felt, as I did, that if I want to drink Pepsi, I will drink Pepsi, but I will not drink Pepsi relabeled as Coke. I drank RC Cola for about year, until real Coke returned as "Coca-Cola Classic", while the new formula became "Coke II" and was never popular. Another disheartening trend of the 80s was toward what I call "match box theaters." This was part of the multiplex trend, which accompanied the new shopping malls, which had begun to be built in the 1970s. As the first multiplexes were being built, some were built with auditoriums which seated perhaps 50 to 75 people and had proportionally smaller screens. It was almost like being at home watching home movies. The fact that these small theaters and Coke II no longer exist is a small tribute to the capitalist system.

Major Cultural and World Events of the 1980s

1980	John Lennon is assassinated on December 9.	Lennon was just 40 years old and extremely popular at the time of his death.
1980	Ted Turner creates CNN news television.	
1984	Bruce Springsteen's *Born in the USA* is the year's best selling album in both the USA and Britain.[58]	
1985	Live Aid earns $60 million for famine relief in Africa.	Two big concerts were performed: one in London and one in Philadelphia. All the musicians and singers performed for free. Over 1.5 billion viewers watched on TV and were asked to pledge money for the cause. Performers included Madonna, Tina Turner, U2, Dire Straits, and Queen.[59]
1986	"Iron Mike" Tyson becomes the youngest ever Heavy Weight World Boxing Champion at the age of 20.	
1988	Stephen R. Covey publishes *The 7 Habits of Highly Effective People.*	

---

[58] Phelps and Courtenay-Thompson, managing editors, "Springsteen strikes international chords", p. 303.

[59] Ibid., "Live aid: music as food of love," p. 304

6

The Road Less Traveled

During the Reagan years I was in my 30s. I had spent my late 20s drifting through life. After completing my bachelor's degree in Colorado, I taught there one year, then wandered for a year. I moved to Arizona in 1978, where I had some old friends and found a climate suitable to my taste. I caught a lucky break that year, which altered my path in life when I applied for a social studies teaching position, didn't get it, but was offered a position teaching math instead. Social studies teaching positions then were almost exclusively reserved for coaches. The number of coaching positions which schools need to fill far exceeds the number of PE positions. The problem then becomes where to put these coaches with PE degrees if they have no other qualifications. They cannot teach English or science or foreign language or math. Social studies—in the late 70s, it was thought that anyone could teach social studies.[60] Schools still have the problem today in regard to the need for coaches, but states have tightened the qualifications requirement for teaching in all fields. I felt like I had been pushed out of the social studies plane (temporarily) with a mathematics parachute. Not everyone could teach math. Math teachers were scarce and in high demand. I stayed with that job for two years before getting restless again.

I decided that I didn't like teaching high school. I chose then to get a master's degree in history, fantasizing about teaching in college. I attended graduate school for a year, then dropped out as my money was running low. I parleyed my experience as a math teacher into tutoring math part-time with two community colleges in Phoenix. Between the two, I could scratch out a living. I liked both jobs and I discovered that I had a knack for explaining mathematical concepts in a clear, understandable form. I also tutored accounting and economics. Eventually I also tutored social

---

[60] Americans today seem to have poor understanding of social issues, but excellent knowledge of football.

studies and English, and I helped students struggling with our Apple 2e computers. I knew how to turn them on and turn them off.

One of the colleges liked my work enough to offer me other jobs so that I could stay at that one campus exclusively. They encouraged me to finish my master's, which I did, and I began teaching history classes in between tutoring. Strangely, my dream of teaching in college had, to some extent, come true. I stayed at that college for five years and loved my work. But I never had a regular fulltime position there; I had multiple part-time jobs, so the pay was always low and there were no benefits. I had taken the road less traveled and I was finding that there is usually a reason why a road is less traveled. Sometimes it's a dead end road. I decided that teaching high school math wasn't so bad after all. I changed course in time; some other boomers I knew never did.

When I looked into getting back to teaching high school, the requirements to teach math had been increased. To qualify now I would need to have 30 math credits. I had 15. But the requirement then was simply 30 credits. They could all be freshman level as long as the total was 30. Between tutoring and teaching, I could take community college math classes. I actually took three of the classes which I had been tutoring. And I took trigonometry, pre-calculus, and calculus. I was almost forty years old and ready to embark on a career. Perhaps I wandered a bit longer than other baby boomers, but many of my generation were also wandering in their thirties.

As I was getting back into teaching high school, I was eager to get my foot in the door and willing to go anywhere. I took a job on the Navajo Reservation in the Northeast corner of Arizona, near the New Mexico line. There I found a rugged, stark beauty which was inspiring. The people were generally friendly, though quiet and reserved. The kids in school were also quiet. I found them easy to teach and fun to work with, though many were behind academically due to somewhat limited English and sporadic attendance. I stayed on the reservation ("the rez") for seven year and learned something of Navajo history and culture.

The Navajos are the largest tribe in the US, rivaled only by the Cherokee. They are on a large reservation which extends into three states—Arizona, New Mexico, and Utah. Scarcity of water is a problem, but the Navajos are happy to be at home on their original land. In 1864 the US government attempted to move the Navajo onto a reservation with other tribes in New Mexico. The migration, which the Navajo call "The Long Walk," was brutal and the conditions on this foreign land were harsh. The Navajo petitioned the federal government to be allowed to return to their homeland, and their petition succeeded in 1868. Since that time the population of Navajos has swelled and the geographical size of their reservation has been expanded four times. The Navajo Reservation now completely encircles that of the Hopi.

Navajos are proud of their unique contribution to America's war effort in World War II. Navajos who were fluent in both Navajo and English were recruited to develop and implement a code for the Marines to use in the Pacific. This Navajo code had the distinction of being the only code on either side of World War II never broken. It also was transmitted with near perfect precision. The success of the code prompted the call for more "Navajo Code Talkers." By the end of the war more than 400 Navajos had served as code talkers in Pacific theater. While the US would certainly have won the war without them, their contribution made it easier and probably saved a lot of American lives.

I had the honor of living right next door to one of the original 29 code talkers who actually developed the code. After the war, they were not allowed to talk about what they had done for several years. The code talker project was classified, because the Marines thought they might use it in the future. Can you imagine, you went to a combat zone and you did this great thing, then you come home and you can't talk about it? Since declassification, several books have been written about the code talkers. One has a photo of my neighbor on the cover. There is also a code talker movie, *Windtalkers,* 2002, but true to Hollywood form, the hero of that movie is a white sergeant (Nicholas Cage) assigned as a bodyguard to a code talker. Each code talker did have a bodyguard assigned. The Marines claimed that the Navajos looked like Japanese to many American Marines, so the bodyguards were assigned to make sure that their fellow Americans did not shoot the code talkers, but many suspected that the bodyguards may have been instructed to shoot the code talker, if it appeared that he might be in danger of being captured. The *Windtalkers* movie focuses attention on this.

"Navajo," I learned, is a name given by the Spanish. The people we call Navajos call themselves "Dine" (din nay). Of course not everybody is the same, but most of the Dine I knew personally were friendly, positive in their outlook, and comfortable walking in two worlds. Unfortunately, unemployment and alcoholism are endemic to the reservation, and economic development is hampered by a brain drain. Many bright, talented Dine leave the reservation for better opportunities elsewhere. Student achievement on average is lower on the rez than other places. I am convinced that the reason for this is mainly poor attendance. I know that when I was teaching on the rez, I was working as hard as I could to raise standards, and I saw many colleagues doing the same. The students generally were not resistant, but they were frequently absent.

What Next?

I thrived on the rez. I got married again and bought a manufactured home. My wife is also a teacher. In the summers, she and I went to college for our ESL (English as a Second Language) endorsements which the school district was warning might become a requirement of all teachers. I learned from this program, and I was working at become a better teacher. Our teaching community lived in a compound, renting our housing from the school district (in my case it was the land for the manufactured home). The teacher compound was a tight community of colleagues and we did a lot of socializing. It was a good life.

But I still wanted something more. I made a crazy decision to pursue a Ph.D. and maybe become a regular, fulltime college history professor. I attended graduate school in the summers for three years, studying history. But to complete the degree, I would be required to attend fulltime continuously at the university for at least a year, then write my dissertation. I had to quit my job on the rez and become a fulltime university student. The university classes I was taking now were very demanding. The amount of reading I was required to do was more than I would ever consider doing voluntarily, and I never have been a fast reader. My wife was understanding, as I had to ignore her quite a bit. I loved the classes and loved what I was reading. I have always enjoyed attending college. My course of study even included more math—graduate level statistics and advanced graduate level statistics. When I finished my coursework, I went back to teaching high school while I was writing my dissertation. I did it! I have a secret to share here. It isn't the smartest people who get Ph.Ds, but the most determined. My training made me a leading scholar relative to a very small detailed part of history. To achieve a Ph.D. one has to specialize, *learning more and more about less and less,* until one gets to the point where he knows *everything about nothing.* The hierarchy of degrees is also amusing. We all know what BS stand for. MS is *more of the same* and Ph.D. is *piled higher and deeper.*

With my history degree completed, I now had another decision to make. With a tight market for college history instructors, I would have to look nationwide for a college position. My wife had found a good job, which she really liked, while I was at the university. I had yanked her off the rez and didn't want to ask her to keep following my half-insane dreams, so I decided to continue teaching high school. I taught high school math during the day and community college history at night. I settled in at a small school in a rural community in which I was the only high school math teacher. This turned out to be the best school at which I ever taught. While I was there our school began to get recognition as being one of the top small, rural public schools in Arizona. I like to think that I was part of that, but I am also happy to report that the tradition of excellence continued after I left.

As for the Ph.D., all that work, financial burden, and sacrifice seemed to have come to nothing. Yet I have never regretted it. It put me in demand as an adjunct faculty member for community college. The year we spent on campus was exciting and is a memory that both Karen and I will always treasure. The personal and intellectual growth I gained was deeply enriching for me. Then in subsequent years, I found that I had the magic letters "P-H-D" which granted me status and advantages I had not anticipated.

The Ph.D. program did change me in one way. I came to enjoy reading. I still read mostly nonfiction. I read about history and social issues. Malcolm Gladwell is among my favorite authors. He has lots of fresh, valuable ideas. I have also begun to enjoy some fiction. I am a fan of Dan Brown because of the way in which he mixes history, over-the-top historical speculation, action, and thought. My dissertation work took me into the world of Theodore Roosevelt and the Rough Riders, and I have read a great deal about him and the American west. I have also read some about World War I and the Middle East. Later experiences stimulate these interests.

7

Complications at the End of the Twentieth Century

I n 1989 Ronald Reagan passed the reins of power onto his vice-president, George H.W. Bush. Bush had a solid resume prior to becoming vice-president, which included a stint as CIA director. He had, in fact, been Reagan's top challenger for the Republican nomination in 1980. Bush's one term presidency is known chiefly for a war he waged against Iraqi dictator Saddam Hussein, when Iraq invaded Kuwait, an oil rich American ally. In Operation Desert Storm, American forces quickly and decisively defeated the invasion force, driving it back into Iraq, a complete success.[61]

To achieve this victory, however, American forces had needed an airbase in the region. Saudi Arabia, an American ally and adversary of Saddam, agreed to allow US military flights into Iraq. This angered some Muslims, among them Osama Bin Laden. As they saw it, the Muslim holy land of Saudi Arabia was being used by a Christian military force, the US, to attack a Muslim country. This may sound like strange logic to western readers, but the collective memory of Arab-Muslims includes centuries of Christian Crusades in attempts to conquer (reconquer) the Holy Land in the east and the Iberian Peninsula (Spain) in the west. Seeing this first Iraq War as a new western Christian crusade, Bin Laden created Al Qaeda. Ironically, Bin Laden, a Saudi national, had spent years in Afghanistan fighting the Soviets and gaining military leadership experience with aid from the United States.

By 1992 when George Bush ran for reelection, the Republicans had held the White House for 12 years. Bill Clinton, of Arkansas, won the Democratic presidential nomination and, in a surprising move, chose a fellow southerner, Tennessee Senator Al Gore, as his running mate. This strategy turned out to be quite brilliant. The

---

[61] Saddam ordered that all the oil wells in Kuwait be set on fire as his army retreated. Putting out the fires took months.

Democratic ticket suddenly had strong appeal in the south and did not suffer any disaffections in the north. The ticket was also helped by the entrance of a third candidate into the race. Ross Perot, a Texas billionaire, ran as an independent, largely self-funded candidate concerned about government deficit spending, a message with greater appeal to Republicans than to Democrats. He received nearly 20 million votes, enough to tip the election in several states. Bill Clinton won the election with only 43% of the popular vote to Bush's 37.5%. The solid Republican south had been fractured temporarily. Besides the home states of Arkansas and Tennessee, Clinton-Gore won Louisiana and Georgia, and the border states of Missouri, Kentucky, and Maryland.[62]

Despite Bill Clinton's personal problems and self-inflicted wounds, his presidency was fairly successful. His eight years were generally years of peace. Where America was militarily involved, it was involved decisively, on the side of right, and as part of NATO operations which intervened to stop genocidal efforts by Serbia in Bosnia and Kosovo.[63] A statue of Bill Clinton stands in the Kosovo capital, Pristina, today in appreciation of the NATO effort there. The good that NATO did in the Balkans under Clinton's direction seems to have been largely forgotten in the US, but it certainly can be pointed to as justification for NATO's existence, as the organization is coming under attack by the current administration.

Clinton's record with regard to legislation is mixed but mostly successful, especially in economic terms. He took a middle road between the philosophical stances of his own Democratic Party and that of the Republicans, negotiating free trade agreements favored by Republicans, which benefited all concerned by stimulating growth in world commerce, but he also unsuccessfully attempted health care reform, a long-time goal of the Democrats. At the end of his tenure, he worked successfully with a Republican Congress. He signed a serious welfare reform bill which he negotiated with the majority Republican legislature. And through bi-partisan efforts, his administration was able to produce a budget surplus.

---

[62] Levy, Michael, "United States presidential election of 1992," www.britanica.com

[63] These attempted genocides were inflicted by Christian Serbians on their Muslim Bosnian and Albanian neighbors. The news media in the US generally described the conflicts as between Christians and Muslims, but these conflicts were not about religion. They were ethnic conflicts.

He had made a miscalculation early when he put his wife, Hillary, in charge of developing a sweeping national health care policy without involving Congressional leaders. He was then unable to get resentful legislators on board for its passage. The Clinton years were marked by economic prosperity, but this was not all due to Clinton policies. It is partially attributable to an economic boom unleashed by the growth of the home computer industry and the internet.

Like everyone else, Karen and I purchased our first home computer and connected to the dial-up internet at this time. My school district was also requiring computer training for all teachers. This was the beginning of my frustrating personal war with computers which is ongoing. Though I use one every day, like everyone else, I still have a healthy distain for them, and I am unhappy to see how computers and iPhones have taken over the lives of young people.

The Clinton years of respectable growth, achievement, relative peace, and American leadership in the world are overshadowed by the impeachment proceedings against the president. A congressional investigation of Clinton's involvement as an investor in the seemingly shady Whitewater Corporation, a real estate firm which went bankrupt, turned up nothing illegal, but the investigation continued and morphed into an investigation of Clinton's personal life. The overzealous prosecutor found out about a sexual affair between Clinton and a young intern at the White House, an episode of which actually occurred in the Oval Office—not really illegal, but certainly in poor taste. Clinton was called before Congress to testify about the incident. Asked about the affair, Clinton denied it under oath. That was the mistake which led to the impeachment. Clinton was charged with lying under oath to Congress. He went through the entire impeachment process. The House voted with a simple majority to send the trial to the Senate. The trial proceeded in the Senate. Because an impeachment trial in the Senate requires a two-thirds vote to convict and Republicans did not have a two-thirds majority, Clinton was acquitted. The voting in both houses was largely along party lines.

We were living in interesting times. Only three presidents have been threatened with impeachment in the entire history of United States, but two of the three impeachment cases were within 25 years of each other, and another president, Reagan, who had actually admitted to a serious crime, was untouched by the process. I think that Clinton should have told Congress that this investigation of his personal life was way out of line and refused to answer. Judging by the vote in both houses, Democrats in Congress seemed to believe the same way. Impeachment, a serious process, which the Constitution reserves for serious crimes, has been subverted to a political process.

OJ

The Clinton impeachment trial was not the trial of my lifetime. It was not even the trial of the decade. Those accolades go to the murder trial of OJ Simpson which many call "the trial of the century." OJ had been a phenomenal football player. He won the Heisman Trophy as the best player in college football with Southern California in 1968. As a professional with the Buffalo Bills, he became the first running back to rush for over 2000 yards in a single season, and he was inducted in the Pro-football Hall of Fame in 1985. After retiring from football, he had a career as a sportscaster and movie actor.

He was accused of the gruesome murders of his ex-wife and a friend, who happened to be with her at the time of the murders. Their throats were slit. The evidence against OJ was strong but not airtight. He implicated himself further by refusing to surrender to police, instead leading them on a "low speed chase." Much of the trial was televised and drew a great deal of interest. In polling, a large majority of white Americans thought he was guilty (myself included), but astonishingly, a majority of African-Americans almost as large believed him to be innocent, clearly indicating a deeper racial divide than I ever imagined. Oddly these murders were too much about black and white to be a black-and-white issue.

The result of the trial was that OJ was acquitted. Some of the jurors interviewed later said that they thought he was guilty, but that they had enough doubt to vote "not guilty." Having been acquitted in criminal court, Simpson found himself the defendant again in a civil case, sued for "wrongful death." The father of the man killed, a Mr. Goldman, had brought the suit. Simpson lost that multi-million dollar suit. Then Goldman offered to let Simpson keep all his money if he would admit to the crime. Simpson refused and the suit bankrupted him. He even lost his Heisman Trophy as part of the payment.

This was not yet the end to this strange saga. Simpson brazenly published a book entitled *If I Had Done It* in which he explained how he could have committed these murders, given all the known facts. Then a few years later he led a group of thugs to break into a Las Vegas hotel room to steal back his Heisman trophy. They were caught. Because of the high value of the trophy, he was convicted of grand larceny, and he went to prison for eight years.[64] The last decade of the twentieth century had indeed been interesting, but the decade to come would change the world.

---

[64] Simpson was released from prison on parole in 2017.

Major Cultural and World Events of the 1990s

1990	Mikhail Gorbachev is awarded the Nobel Peace Prize	The prize is richly deserved.
1993	The European Union is officially created.	
1993	Nelson Mandela is awarded the Nobel Peace Prize.	Mandela leads the campaign against apartheid and for subsequent reconciliation efforts. This is made all the more extraordinary because Mandela had been imprisoned by the apartheid regime of South Africa for more than two full decades.
1994	Nelson Mandela is elected as South Africa's first black President.	
1997	J.K. Rowling publishes *Harry Potter and The Philosopher's Stone*, the first of her Harry Potter novels.	
1998	Mark McGuire sets the new single season major league home run record at 70. Sammy Sosa also broke Babe Ruth's record by hitting 66 home runs that same year.	
1998	The Chicago Bulls win their sixth NBA championship of the 1990s all with star player Michael Jordan.	
1999	The Euro is introduced as the new European currency.	

8

A New World in a New Millennium

"W" and the Day the World Changed

Bill Clinton's presidency had been successful enough for his loyal vice-president, Al Gore, to win the Democratic nomination for president in 2000. Gore was opposed by George W. Bush, the son of former President George H. W. Bush. (School children will be driven crazy by this in the future.) Bush, the younger, is often referred to simply as "W." The election was very close. When it was all over Gore had actually won the popular vote. The electoral vote hinged on Florida, where the voting was neck-and-neck. When the ballots were first counted, Bush appeared to have won, but there was an irregularity. Florida used a ballot wherein voters punched out the chad for their choice. Many of these chads did not punch all the way off but were left hanging instead. When counted electronically, some "hanging chads" did not register a vote. The Governor of Florida, Jeb Bush, brother of "W" Bush, wanted to accept the count as recorded. Gore wanted a manual recount. The obvious intension of the voters, I would argue, should be what counts. The issue was taken to the Supreme Court which ruled to let the count stand at which time Gore conceded the election to Bush.

George W. Bush was not a great intellect but honest and well-intentioned. He would have been an adequate president in normal times. No one could have imagined the gargantuan challenge that this new president and America would face on September 11, 2001 and how our lives would be changed. This day, like the day John Kennedy was shot, is seared into the minds of all of us who experienced it. I remember that I was driving to work; I stopped for coffee at a convenience store, as I always did. I always listened to Paul Harvey on the radio on my way to work. He came on at 6:30 AM and his show lasted about ten minutes. At the very end of the Paul Harvey Show that day, Paul said with a voice of bewilderment, "This just in. It seems that someone has flown a plane into the World Trade Center." At that moment I arrived at my school, went inside, and began reviewing my lessons for the day. Shortly after that, one of my colleagues came into my room and asked if I heard what was going on. "No." He then told me to turn on my radio. That's when I started getting the news—one plane, one tower, then two planes, both towers, then both towers falling, thousands dead; the Pentagon assailed. We had classes that day, but everyone was in shock and we were listening to the news all day. I tried to teach like this was a normal day in order not to alarm the students. Others handled it differently.

Our world had changed. Everyone would be changed in some way, some more than others. The President showed leadership by going to ground zero immediately. He also quickly announced the details that were known, including that the attack had been planned by Osama Bin Laden and that he was holed up in Afghanistan under the protection of the Taliban government. The President demanded that Bin Laden be turned over to the US. The US invasion of Afghanistan was an entirely appropriate response when the Afghan government, under the Taliban, refused to give him up. In the beginning, the war went well, the Taliban was ejected from the capital and Taliban fighters retreated into the mountains between Afghanistan and Pakistan. Afghanistan appeared to be moving toward democracy. Unfortunately, Bin Laden got away.

My own life would take a profound change. As I saw it, I had a part to play in this somehow. I may have taken the attack more personally than most people. I and some colleagues organized a charity dinner with proceeds going to families of the victims of the attack. I also began looking for ways to be directly involved in the response to the attack. I appealed to be allowed to join the army and wrote to my congressman and senators for support. I was over 50, so this was unrealistic, and of course it failed. I looked for every possibility. As I saw it, my country and the world were in crisis, and I had to do something. In desperation and with the view that to do anything is better than to do nothing, I volunteered for the Peace Corps and my wife agreed to volunteer with me.

As we moved ahead with a long, cumbersome Peace Corps application process (as it was then), the United States, under President Bush, with the Afghan War under control, became involved in another war, this one with Iraq under the pretext that Saddam Hussein had "weapons of mass destruction," a pretext which proved false. The armies of Saddam, though large in number, were easily defeated, but then the real war in Iraq began—a civil war which the Bush administration should have foreseen but didn't. The president appeared to have planned to impose American style democracy in Iraq. Democracy, however, was not compatible with the Iraqi society which was deeply divided between Sunnis and Shias. Saddam, a Sunni, had suppressed the Shia majority. American style democracy would mean that the Shia, about 65% of the population, could now get even with the Sunni, while monopolizing government jobs themselves. The Sunnis rebelled. Civil war followed. That civil war dragged on with the US in the middle, trying to restore stability. Resources and attention were being concentrated on Iraq, while the Taliban was regaining strength in Afghanistan. Iraq was a mess, and Afghanistan was sliding in the same direction.

Now, more than a decade later, Afghanistan has the Taliban in control of parts of the country and staging frequent terrorist bombings in Kabul; Al Qaeda has been crippled, largely by the freezing of Bin Laden's bank accounts and other funding sources; and Bin Laden, himself, has been killed; but the world as a whole is less safe because ISIS, which did not exist before the invasion of Iraq, grew out of the chaos and anger created by the Iraqi Civil War.

Jordan, the Peace Corps, and What I Learned

In the midst of all this, Karen and I were struggling to get into the Peace Corps. The process took almost two years, because we both failed the physical on the basis of minor health issues, and we had to wait an extra year. We had volunteered to go anywhere in the world. When our appointment did come through, we were assigned to Jordan. I was delighted and Karen was apprehensive. For me this was incredibly lucky. I really wanted to go somewhere where my efforts might make, at least, a small difference. With the Iraqi War raging on Jordan's border and America's standing in the Middle East diminishing as a result, Jordan was the perfect place for me. Add to that the fact that the 9-11 attackers were all from the Arab Middle East, there appeared to be an added urgency in helping to create dialogue between the west and the Middle East. Karen was concerned about the possibility of anti-American feeling in the region.

We were to report to Washington, DC on July 5, 2005. Karen and I arrived a few days earlier to tour the capital and say goodbye the Karen's relatives, who lived nearby in Pennsylvania. We were in DC for the Fourth of July fireworks. After the two day induction process, our group of 32 volunteers was on our way to Jordan. Naturally most in the group were young. There were, however, a half dozen of us senior citizens ranging in age from forty-six to seventy-five. The oldest member of the group had served in the Peace Corps three times previously. The young people were all well-educated and intelligent. Many had studied Arab culture; I had not. I soon found that most of my colleagues were more widely-traveled than I and sophisticated beyond their years. During training I often felt that I had lots of catching up to do. But I liked these people, and I soon felt that I was on a great adventure—the time of my life.

Older readers will remember that the Peace Corps had been founded in 1961 by the presidential order of John F. Kennedy. When I was young and idealistic, I would have considered joining the Peace Corps. But by the time I finished high school, the magic of Camelot had faded under the dark cloud of Vietnam. I served my two years in Lyndon's legions. Now, more than thirty years later, I felt I was where I belonged—with Kennedy's kids. Karen and I were realistic about the job ahead. Anything we would do here would make very little difference in the world, but making little difference is better than making no difference at all.

Our experience in Jordan was eye-opening and life changing. Karen and I were not world travelers. I had been to Mexico, Canada, and Ireland—that's it. Karen had traveled more than I, but always as a tourist. Our cross-cultural experience was limited to the years we had spent teaching on the Navajo Reservation. Now we were on the other side of the world, immersed in the Arab-Muslim culture. Fortunately, the Peace Corps eases volunteers into the shallow end of the pool before allowing them to swim on their own. We were set-up to live with a family for ten weeks during training—a husband and wife with eight children. (Large families are the norm in Jordan.) Our homestay hosts were wonderful, and we remain good friends today. But we really did have a lot to learn.

Their house was like a small castle to me—extremely large and rather beautiful. It had three levels. The first level was used as a barn for the animals. They had lots of sheep. They also had goats, chickens, turkeys, rabbits, and pigeons. The second and third levels of the house both had a long hallway, many large rooms, and a terrace. The roof was flat and had a wall waist high all around it. I soon learned that this house was fairly typical, except for the animals on the first floor. Houses were very large because families were large and a single house often accommodated multiple generation of an extended family. Houses were often constructed and expanded over many years as families grew. Each level of a house would be constructed individually with pillars and rebar sticking out so that when the family grew the next level could be easily added. Once three levels were constructed then the house was complete. One and two story houses with pillars and rebar sticking out were a common sight in Jordan.

I am a picky eater, so I frustrated our hosts in the beginning. But Jordanian food was not difficult to adapt to. I really enjoyed the Jordanian breakfast. For breakfast you have a spread of many tasty choices which include falafels, a tomato dish, fried eggs, hummus, a sweet, French fries, thyme, olives, and olive oil. Silverware is not used. Instead everyone has flatbread. You tear off pieces and use them to scoop whatever you want. Sweet tea is served with the meal. For a feast, the national dish, mansef, is prepared. This is a bed of rice with chicken or mutton and peanuts on top. It is served on a large communal tray placed on a plastic sheet on the floor. Diners squat or kneel or sit on the side of one foot (which I could never manage to do) around the tray. Hot yogurt sauce is poured over the rice. Diners eat using their right hands by mushing the rice and some chicken together into something resembling a ball and popping it into their months. People do use both hands to pull pieces of chicken apart, but only the right hand otherwise. (The left hand and a hose are used to clean oneself after going to the bathroom.)

I found most of the Peace Corps training to be interesting and valuable though some of the younger volunteers made fun of it. Language training was the largest component, but we also had classes designed for cultural awareness and classes to train volunteers for their specific assignments, like teaching English. The history and culture classes were helpful to me in understanding, not only Jordan, but the entire Middle East.

I once heard an American speak of Jordan as "a made-up country." It is true that no such country existed before World War I. That war gave birth to the modern Middle East and all the problems associated with it. The war, having begun in August 1914, had ground to a bloody and costly stalemate, and British leaders became desperate to make some breakthrough. Secret negotiations with Hussein, Sharif of Mecca, resulted in a 1916 alliance between the Arabs and the British, as the Arabs sought to throw off the domination of the Ottoman Empire. The British promised the Arabs that upon successful conclusion of the war, the Arabs would have an independent country. Unfortunately the British were making conflicting promises. They promised their French ally that they would share the Middle East essentially equally with them, and they promised the Jews that they would have a homeland established in the Middle East in exchange for Jewish support of the war effort.

In the wrangling after the war, the British attempted to satisfy all their war partners. Hussein was given the Hejaz, the part of the Arabian Peninsula centered around Mecca. (A few year later the Saudis overthrew his government and established Saudi Arabia.) Hussein's oldest son, Feisal, who had actually led the revolt, was at first made King of Syria.[65] When the French objected to this kingdom in their sphere of influence, Feisal became King of Iraq. In attempting to keep their promise to the Jewish people, the British established a protectorate in Palestine which they declared would become a Jewish state. The British protectorate of Transjordan was carved out of the Arab land to the immediate east of Palestine to provide a kingdom (under British authority) for Feisal's younger brother, Abdullah, to rule over and a place to which Arabs unhappy with the thought of living under Jewish rule might migrate. The lands of Palestine and Transjordan had both been sparely populated at that time. Abdullah was accepted as king of Transjordan by the natives of the region because his family members were direct descendants from the Prophet, Muhammad.

Transjordan became the independent Hashemite Kingdom of Jordan in 1946. Abdullah's grandson, King Hussein, forged it into a nation. Hussein was king from 1952 until his death in 1999. He was very much loved by his people, and he is called "the father of his country." He did much to develop and modernize the country while steering it in the direction of tolerance and moderation, as much of the rest of the Middle East remained radically conservative and intolerant. Since Hussein's death, his western educated son, Abdullah II, has continued to pursue his father's policies and to work tirelessly for peace in the Middle East. As a result of the efforts

---

[65] T. E. Lawrence, Lawrence of Arabia, had been Feisal's partner in their exploits against the Ottomans. Lawrence later accompanied Feisal and supported Arab demands at the Versailles Peace Conference of 1919.

of Hussein and Abdullah II, Jordan wields greater influence and prestige than its size and population would otherwise command, and the people native to Jordan proudly identify themselves as "Jordanian."[66] I should also note that Jordan is one of only two Arab countries which actually has a peace agreement with Israel.

Jordan, however, is not a democracy, though it has democratic elements, chiefly, a bicameral legislature and a constitution which protects the rights of minorities and women. But the prime minister is appointed by the king, as are all members of the Senate. The king, himself, has broad executive power, and a large internal security force, a secret police, is active, spying on citizens throughout the country. This sounds strange, but Jordan is a country with serious security threats all around. Over half of the population consists of Palestinian refugees, many of whom have shown to be not particularly loyal to Jordan. In 1970, Palestinians challenged King Hussein by staging a civil war in which they were defeated. Palestinian leaders were subsequently expelled from the country. Nevertheless, Palestinian-Jordanians still represent a possible internal threat. And no Middle East country has more conflicts on its borders than Jordan. Bordering countries are Syria, Iraq, Palestine, Israel, and Saudi Arabia; and Lebanon is close. All have their own conflicts and problems. When I was in Jordan, there were a million Iraq War refugees in the country. Most of them have since returned to Iraq. But now Jordan has a similar number of Syrian refugees for which to care. Given the assortment of existential threats, the secret police force in Jordan is a practical necessity.

Jordan, I learned, is resource poor. It has no exploitable oil deposits, little mineral wealth of any kind, and a large expanse of barren desert. As a result the government encourages "the knowledge economy." Young men are encouraged to become educated to become doctors or engineers or computer technologists. The young man who fails to qualify for these professions might still be a teacher. Young women in Jordan are not discouraged from education, but they are not pushed as much as boys. However, if a young woman qualifies, she can be a doctor, a pilot, or anything she wants to be in Jordan. Most bright young women who enter a profession become teachers. Because Jordan produces a large number of

---

[66] I know this from the many Jordanians with who I came in contact. However, those people living in Jordan who are refugees from Palestine might not be as enthusiastic about being "Jordanian."

professionals, many professional men find employment outside the country. The remittances they send back are an important component of the Jordanian economy. The most important part of the economy, however, seems to be agriculture despite a scarcity of water.

Water is a precious thing in the semi-arid land of Jordan. Most of the wells are very deep and many villages are not hooked into a well system, but rather receive their water by truck on a once a week basis. It is very important for these people to conserve. Many people have a catchment system for rainwater on their roofs. According to an official Jordanian government source I found, the average Jordanian uses about sixty liters of water a day compared to 300 liters which the average American uses. Most of the population of Jordan lives in or close to the mountains of the northwest where rainfall is more frequent than in the other three-fourths of the country. This land is farmed, while the desert lands are mostly used for sheep herding.

I have read that there is a kind of aversion to manual labor throughout the Arab world. In Jordan the official unemployment rate was twenty percent when I was there. The actual rate of unemployment could be much higher since "farmer" is a term that can apply to any young man at home in rural Jordan. Yet most construction work is done by Egyptians, and most of the domestic laborers are Filipinos. Many Jordanian computer experts, doctors, and teachers go to work in rich countries like Saudi-Arabia where no one among the native population wants to work at all. When you think about it, Jordan and the Middle East are not really much different from the United States which is a magnet for workers from Mexico and Central America.

When our Peace Corps training ended, we moved to a different village for our service. The Peace Corps set us up with housing there too. I don't mean to imply that Peace Corps service in Jordan was easy. It was challenging, especially immediately after training when our actual service began. The village to which Karen and I were assigned had had one Peace Corps volunteer years before, but the Peace Corps had pulled out of Jordan at the beginning of the first Gulf War (1990) and was only now reestablishing itself fifteen years later. So, the two Americans in the village were like extraterrestrial visitors. At first I could not walk across campus at my school without being mobbed by curious boys. Yet after school we were very much alone that first week. On the first night that we were in the village, Karen woke me to say that there was lots of noise outside and I should go out and investigate. I ignored her, rolled over, and went back to sleep. We learned the next day that there had been an earthquake alert for the village that night. No one really knew us, so no one took responsibility for alerting us. I can't say that I ever knew why our landlord, who lived above us, didn't wake us. Most likely this was because he didn't speak English, and we spoke very little Arabic, so he would have had a challenge getting the bewildered Americans up in the middle of the night.

That wasn't the scariest thing for us in the beginning either. About two months into our service, I got a call in the middle of the night from our PC country director alerting me to the fact that there had been a bombing of a large western hotel in Amman and about 80 people were dead. It turned out that this was an Al Qaeda terrorist attack. The people killed were all Jordanians and almost all from a single wedding party. There was an immediate buzz among members of my PC group. The question was "Who's leaving?" Within a week, five members of the group decided to resign and go home, citing the feeling of not being safe. I was staying. I made a commitment for two years, so I was staying for two years. Karen and I talked it over. I told her that I was staying and she could go if she wanted. She had no hesitation about staying. In truth, I could not have gone home if I wanted to. Everyone at my school in the US and everyone in the town where we had lived knew all about our Jordanian adventure. As I was leaving for this noble cause, I was a commencement speaker at graduation. And Karen and I had our picture and story on the front page of the local newspaper.

As for those who decided to leave, I think they were frustrated with Jordanian village life, the difficulties of the work, and difficulties of integration into the local communities. The bombing gave them an excuse to leave. For those of us assigned as English teachers, our teaching assignments were quite difficult. Many of the students were disruptive and difficult to control. Of course, many of them were turned-off because they could not understand us. Some of the Jordanian teachers were helpful to us with this, but some were not helpful at all. I had no way to go but forward, and that was a good thing.

Adjusting to the culture did take some time, but it was not as difficult as one might think. Jordan is not super-conservative, like

Saudi-Arabia, but you won't see short skirts (or any leg) in Jordan. Most Muslim women in Jordanian villages do wear the hijab, the head scarf, but only a very few wear the niqab, or face vail. Men and women do live separate lives. After a while, Karen and I were established and accepted in our village. Now we would often be invited to parties. When we arrived at the door, a man would escort me upstairs to the men's party and a woman would escort Karen to the women's party. After the party, we would walk home together and talk about the parties we had attended. Everything is separated like that in Jordan. I taught at the boys' school; Karen taught at the girls' school.

As I struggled to gain acceptance as a teacher, I found salvation in an unexpected way. My school put up a basketball hoop, and I began playing basketball after school with a few of the boys. Basketball is not a popular sport in Jordan. Everybody plays football (soccer), not basketball. I am really not a basketball player, but I could play a little then and I know the rules. I played almost every afternoon and taught the students the rules, along with my lame moves. As time went on, more students joined the group. Eventually we had up to twenty boys playing, taking turns on the court. I gained lots of allies among the boys as a result. With this base, I made slow, steady progress in the classroom and in time I gained real acceptance. (Many of the boys who played were good athletes, so my days as a basketball star didn't last long.)

Peace Corps volunteers are directed to serve entire communities in which they are placed, not just a school or single organization. Karen and I were seldom bored. When it became known that Americans were in the village offering free English lessons, we found ourselves quite busy. I also picked up a pleasant job as an English advisor at a nature reserve nearby which drew foreign tourists. And I made myself available to anyone who wanted to discuss anything—mostly politics—with the village American. People in Jordan tend to stay up late, so I would sometimes get calls at 10:30 or 11 by some acquaintance who had a friend who wanted to talk. Okay, yes, so I would get out of bed, get dressed, and be ready for a car to come and pick me up. Then I would be out somewhere for an hour or two. Great fun. Karen tutored children in our home and picked up an extra assignment too. Her actual specialty in America had been as a teacher of visually impaired students. With this expertise, she was recruited to help one day a week at a Christian school which was the only school in the country specializing in serving the visually impaired along with sighted children. We came to understand the old slogan of the Peace Corps, "the toughest job you'll ever love." We made great friends and had the time of our lives.

Islam is the official religion of Jordan, and the royal family, as I mentioned earlier, is actually descended from the Prophet Muhammad. At the same time, Christianity is tolerated and protected, though proselytizing of Christianity is a crime. Ten percent of the seats in the Jordanian legislature are designated for Christians, though the Christian population is more like five percent. Muslims consider Christians to be fellow "people of the book" and Jesus to be a prophet of God, second only to Muhammad. Other religions are officially tolerated, though the locals may be somewhat hostile to those, especially in the rural communities. We soon found that Sunni Muslims pray five times a day. As a result, the religion is central to their lives and always on their minds. Because nearly everyone is Muslim, a kind of group-think seems apparent. Islam is embraced as the absolute truth with no equivocation. The Koran is itself a sacred object to be treated with the utmost reverence. It is never to be placed on the floor. It is to be kept on the highest shelf. It is considered to be the exact world of God. As Christians, we were accepted and welcomed, but being an atheist would not have been an option.

Muslims are commanded to invite others to the faith. When I was new to the village, I had several people lecture me on Islam, and Karen and I were each given a copy of the Koran with English translation. But people weren't really pushy about it. People in the village soon accepted that we would not convert, and they were perfectly okay about it—all except for one guy, a fellow teacher, whom I had to see every day. He just could not understand how I could reject Islam after he had told me all about it. He confronted me on the issue almost daily, becoming more aggressive by the day for over a week, until a bunch of the other teachers went to him and demanded that he knock it off. Months later he apologized.

In all the discussions in which I participated, we did not talk much about religion, but politics was a topic of intense interest. The Kingdom of Jordan is an American ally and one of only two Arab countries which has a peace treaty with Israel, but the citizens of Jordan generally were not fans of US foreign policy, and they were especially not fans of Israel. I had lots of interesting discussions by which I learned quite a bit, while explaining about American ideas and politics. Perhaps, the most enlightening question I was asked was "Why does America support the Shias in Iraq and the Sunnis in Iran?" When I heard this question, I had not yet realized the extent of the rivalry between Shias and Sunnis and how it was the central issue driving the civil war in Iraq. In other conversations, I discovered that Saddam Hussein had a great many sympathizers in Jordan because he had been a fellow Sunni exerting Sunni control in Iraq, a mostly Shia country. It was during our time in Jordan than Saddam was hanged. This was the only time I felt a little apprehensive and unwelcome in Jordan. Most of the Jordanians understandably had a very low opinion of George W. Bush.

Jordanians are generally knowledgeable about most political facts, but some have a victim mentality. I was once asked if I knew that the US had killed 100,000 people in Iraq. I became slightly incensed. I had to say, "Wait a minute! I know that 100,000 people have been killed in Iraq. If you say that much of this is the fault off the US, I might concede that you have a point. But Americans are dying in Iraq, trying to keep Iraqis from killing Iraqis. Would you die to keep Americans from killing Americans?" This got no response but ended the discussion abruptly. Americans, too, see the world through a cultural filter which blinds them to truths which might be apparent to people of other cultures. Seeing beyond ones cultural filter requires extra effort, but without making the effort, we are all prisoners in Plato's Cave.

The Sunni-Shia rivalry is important for all Americans to know about because it is among the main driving forces of Middle East politics. Simply stated, Iran is the leading Shia country, while Saudi Arabia is the leading Sunni country. Shias are thought to be more conservative and religiously driven than Sunnis, but the Saudis are Wahhabi Sunnis, possibly the most radical Muslims of all. Fifteen out of nineteen of the 9-11 hijackers were Saudi. Shia followers make up most of the population of Iran, about 65% of the Iraqis, most of the Yemenese, and constitute significant minorities in Lebanon and Syria. Bashar Al Assad in Syria belongs to a branch of Shia and is attempting to rule over a country which was mostly Sunni. Hezbollah in Lebanon is a Shia organization funded and directed by Iran. But Al Qaeda and ISIS claim Sunni beliefs. Hamas is more a political entity with little religious affiliation. Sunnis claim to be more outward looking and scientifically oriented than the more spiritual Shias. Jordan is mostly Sunni. The Palestinians are Sunni, as are most Kuwaitis, Egyptians, and the people of the UAE.

My personal belief is that the religious fanaticism of Saudi Arabia is as dangerous as that of Iran. The restrictions on women are more severe in Saudi-Arabia than in Iran, and Iran has democratic elections; Saudi Arabia does not.

Everyone I met in Jordan had an interest in what was happening in Iraq but a much greater interest in the issue of Israel and Palestine. The big cities of Jordan have large concentrations of Palestinian refugees, but it appears that sympathy for Palestinians would be strong even without this fact. Through many conversations, I came to realize that the Palestinian issue is a needle constantly poking at and irritating Muslims, especially the Arabs. President G. W. Bush was wrong by thinking that he could transform the Middle East by starting in Iraq. Transformation is possible, but it must start with Israel-Palestine. If a just peace can be arranged here, the entire Middle East can be transformed. Unfortunately, Israeli leaders seem to have discarded that last, best hope.

The Oslo Accords nearly achieved a comprehensive peace settlement, but that hope was allowed to slip away because small minded men on both sides lacked common sense or courage. The Accords were signed in 1993 between the government of Israel and the leaders of the Palestinians. The essential agreement was that the Palestinians recognized Israel's right to exist, and Israel would allow an independent Palestinian state which would consist of most of the West Bank and Gaza.[67] There were three items of contention which were to be resolved within five years, so the entire package was to be done by the end of 1998.

Since 1993 the Israelis have shown clearly that they are totally unwilling to make any compromise on any issue, and the Palestinian leadership has shown itself to be incapable of negotiating or leading effective peaceful protest. All three items left for future negotiations have all been stonewalled by Israel. Issue number one was the right to return or receive compensation for land lost by Palestinians who fled Israel or Israeli occupied land during the Arab-Israeli Wars. Number two was the status of East Jerusalem. East Jerusalem and the West Bank had been part of Jordan and were seized by Israel in the Six Day War of 1967. Jordan has since agreed to relinquish

---

[67] Because this was a major breakthrough, PLO leader Yasser Arafat, a murderous criminal to many, and Israeli leaders Shimon Perez and Yitzhak Rabin all received the Nobel Peace Prize in 1994. Rabin would be assassinated by a countryman, meeting the same fate fellow peacemaker Anwar Sadat had met in 1981.

its claim in favor of the Palestinians. The Palestinians wanted, and still want, East Jerusalem returned and hope to make it the capital of the proposed Palestinian state. It should be noted that Jerusalem is holy to Muslims, as well as Jews and Christians, and all of Jerusalem was ruled by the Muslims for most of the previous 1200 years. Israel has given no consideration to the return of East Jerusalem. On the contrary, the Israelis moved their capitol from Tel Aviv to Jerusalem and have since stated that Jerusalem is one city and will never be divided.[68] The third item was the problem of Israeli settlements in the West Bank; would they be dismantled? No, in direct defiance of the spirit of the Oslo Accords, Israel is continuing to build new settlements in the West Bank and expand existing ones. Israel has even boldly constructed some Israeli only highways linking the Israeli villages in the West Bank.

While good models of effective peaceful protests exist (Gandhi, Martin Luther King, Mandela), the Palestinian Authority (Fatah Party), which claims leadership of the Palestinian people, does not do enough, as the continuing cycle of violence and hatred swirls about Israel-Palestine, and ordinary Israelis don't seem to make much effort to protest the injustices of their own government either. Hamas, which is in power in Gaza, extolls hatred, violence, and denial.

On Monday, May 14, 2018 President Trump announced that the United States would be the first country in the entire world to move its embassy to Jerusalem, implying American approval for the occupation and appropriation of Arab East Jerusalem by Israel. I see this as a stain on the United States. But there is plenty of shame to go around in Israel-Palestine—the Israelis for their intransience, greed, and stubbornness; Fatah in the West Bank for failure to negotiate or lead effective protest; and Hamas in Gaza for consistently offering only hatred and violence with no real thought of any intelligent solution. If anything good comes of the embassy move, it will be because the world now knows not to depend on the

---

[68] By announcing that he intended to move the American Embassy from Tel Aviv to Jerusalem, President Trump appeared to indicate that the US would not be neutral in the Palestinian-Israeli Conflict. As of the time of this writing, no other country has an embassy in Jerusalem out of respect for Palestinian rights. The General Assembly of the United National voted 128 to 9 to condemn Trump's proclamation.

United States to play any constructive role in solving the problems of Israel-Palestine.

When I was in Jordan, the Oslo process was still alive though barely, and the Jordanian king, Abdullah II, was a strong proponent of moving it forward. He made big news in Jordan when he went to the United States for a week to lobby for support of the process. The highlight of his visit was a speech he gave to a joint session of Congress outlining what needed to be done. That speech was carried in its entirety on Jordanian television. I had satellite TV in my house and could get two of the three major US network daily primetime television news shows. I was very interested in seeing what their coverage would be. Neither even mentioned the speech to Congress. I found this to be curious because I don't believe that joint sessions of Congress are that common, and when Israeli leaders have spoken before such joint sessions, they have always received major news coverage. In the whole week that King Abdullah was in the US, I heard only one very brief mention of his visit on only one of the two networks without any mention of the business for which he came. The really big news that the networks were covering in detail that week was about an astronaut driving cross-country, while wearing a diaper to confront her boyfriend's other lover. Some of my Jordanian friends always asserted that the American media is controlled by Israeli sympathizers. I used to think this was ridiculous, but the example above tends to support the theory. At the very least this calls into question decision making about what news to cover. I would suggest that responsible news coverage should more carefully consider what people need to know as much as what people want to know. Ideally this could even mean better long-run network ratings as people might come to see the importance of relevant information.

One thing is for certain now. Oslo is dead. A whole new reset will have to occur to present any hope of peace in the Middle East, and the US needs to either play a positive role or get out of the way. America has been the great enabler for all Israeli intransience. We provide generous military aid and the best military equipment. Per **capita** US aid to Israel, incidentally, is higher than for any third world country. We also provide cover in the Security Council of the United Nations, often standing alone with our veto of even verbal condemnation of any Israeli action.

The Peace Corps program has three goals: (1) to provide technical assistance to developing countries; (2) to promote person-to-person diplomacy—direct contact between American volunteers and native citizens; and (3) awareness of other countries and cultures through returned volunteers sharing their experiences. I returned from Jordan determined to raise consciousness about the Middle East and the issue of Palestine. That was in 2007. Oslo was not yet dead at that time. I spoke in schools, to civic groups, in libraries, to anyone who might have any interest. I haven't completely given up on the cause, because without hope of a Palestinian settlement there is no hope of any permanent Middle East peace. In the US, a coalition of extremists, Christian and Jewish, supporting the idea of "greater Israel" stands in the way to progress. Their belief is that all of this land, including all of Jerusalem and the West Bank, was given to the Jews by God more than 2000 years ago and, therefore, none of this land should be returned to Arabs even though few Jews lived in the region for 2000 years while Arabs have family histories here which go back many centuries. The "greater Israel" supporters, conservative Christians and radical Jews, do not respect the fundamental human principle that all people are equal. This is indecency to which decent people must stand in opposition regardless of their religion or nationality.

While I was in Jordan, I was reading a lot about the conflict, trying to understand all aspects of it. In my last months in Jordan, Jimmy Carter published a book explaining the conflict, the Oslo Accords, and the efforts and frustrations involved in the quest for peace. It's a good book, but there are lots of good books written about this topic which have been ignored. This book was far from ignored because it was brilliantly titled, *Palestine: Peace, Not Apartheid*. Israel's many defenders in the US and in Israel were incensed, countering that Israel is not an apartheid state. Whether or not that is true, Carter was not writing about Israel; he was writing about Palestine--the West Bank. The controversy and opposition about the title was probably better publicity than any paid publicity campaign could ever have been.

Israel's defenders no doubt felt under siege when another bomb was dropped on them just a few months later, as *The Israel Lobby and U.S. Foreign Policy* by John Mearsheimer and Stephen Walt hit bookstores.[69] Carter, Mearsheimer, and Walt were all attacked mercilessly. In their book, Measheimer and Walt warned that the American Israel Political Affairs Committee (AIPAC), a pro-Israeli lobbying group, exerts an enormous amount of pressure to influence American politicians to act in ways beneficial to Israel, which may not be beneficial to the United States. AIPAC apologists are quick to point out that the organization does nothing illegal and contributes no money to any politician or political party. True, AIPAC only provides information. The trick is that AIPAC has a large number of members, many of whom are wealthy and do contribute to candidates. So, if any politician says anything construed as anti-Israeli or insufficiently pro-Israeli, AIPAC quickly reports the affront, and that politician finds his opponent in the next election extremely well-funded by donors from all over the country. To take even a mild stand against such things as illegal Israeli settlements in the West Bank will be political suicide. So, much of the pro-Israeli rhetoric which frequently flows from Washington is not patriotism, but pandering.[70]

Travels in Jordan and Africa

Despite my serious concerns and serious work, I had a great time in Jordan and some incredible vacations. Karen and I toured ancient Roman ruins at Jerash and Umm Qais, a mediaeval Muslim castle at Ajloun, and the ancient Nabataean site of Petra that was carved out of solid rock in a time that pre-dated the Roman conquest of the area. Petra has since been voted as one of the "Wonders of the World," and it is the site of the climactic scenes in *Indiana Jones and the Last Crusade*. All these places are within Jordan, and all but Petra were short day trips from where we lived. However, our greatest vacation, the vacation of a lifetime, was in Africa.

We started in Cairo, where we stayed with a friend. We went to see the Pyramids and the Sphinx at Giza. I passed up the opportunity to ride a camel at that time for the thrill of horseback riding, which I hadn't done for years. Karen got the camel. We also saw the King

---

[69] John Mearsheimer, Political Scientist of the University of Chicago and Stephen Walt, Professor of International Relations at the Kennedy School of Government at Harvard University.

[70] Politicians also fear the Christian right which is also insistent in supporting Greater Israel.

Tut exhibit with all the lavish gold at the National Museum in Cairo. Tut, the boy king, was not an important pharaoh, but his was the only pharaoh's tomb discovered with all the treasures intact, untouched by looters. The Tut display was so impressive that one wonders what kinds of riches would have been buried with a more important pharaoh likes Rameses II. From Cairo we flew to Luxor and saw all the huge statues that were right out of my textbooks. While in Luxor we visited the Valley of the Kings, where we bought tickets to go inside three of the tombs. I was amazed by how vivid and well preserved the colors were in the tombs. That was phase one of our vacation!

From Egypt we flew to Nairobi, Kenya and took a life-threatening ride with a speeding driver dodging craters in the road to Arusha, Tanzania. There we went on a picture taking safari to three national parks—three days, two nights with the safari company insisting on doing everything for us, setting up the tent, cooking our meals, and doing the cleanup. The vehicle was a kind of jeep with an open roof for viewing and photography. The first day at Tarangire National Park was most memorable for a bad reaction Karen had to the anti-malaria medicine which the Peace Corps had provided us. We were out in the park and Karen got violently ill. "Stop, I have to get out right now," she said. The poor tour guide said, "No! No one can get out here! It's very dangerous." But Karen insisted until the guide agreed to stop the vehicle and let her out very close to the jeep. I went out with her to watch for animals. Karen emptied her stomach while I watched movement in the grass carefully. I didn't tell her at the time what I was watching--a large snake. I would estimate it as at least twenty feet long and between one and two feet in diameter. I don't think it was big enough to consume either of us, but I wouldn't gamble my life on that. I watched it carefully, and it remained what I hoped was a safe distance away. After we were back in the vehicle, I told Karen what I saw. Funny thing though, that was the only snake I saw on the whole trip.

The tour was nicely designed so that each day was more spectacular than the previous day. The second day was at Lake Manyara and the last day was at Ngorongora, which is a collapsed volcanic crater. On the safari we saw literally hundreds, maybe thousands, of wild animals, and we saw every wild animal that Africa has except a cheetah. But we got up close to almost everything else in the safety of the jeep with an open roof, really close to elephants. After returning to Arusha, we took a bus to the coast where we stayed at a resort on the Indian Ocean that happened to be owned by a former Peace Corps colleague. We enjoyed our own peaceful, personal beach before traveling to Dar es Salaam and a flight back to Jordan.

Back in the USA

After concluding my service, I arrived back in the US in August 2007 and went back to teaching math. That first year back I taught in a large urban school, but it wasn't for me. I took a pay cut to teach in a small rural school east of Phoenix the following year. This was more my style, but I still was not completely readjusted. The common core (national) curriculum was being adopted in Arizona and I was not comfortable with it. In math anyway, I saw the common core as a giant step backwards. I certainly could be wrong about this; I didn't stick around long enough to give it a fair chance. But the common core was recently abandoned in Arizona as a failed experiement.

The rural school at which I taught was a good experience overall. The kids were nice, the faculty was good, and the administration was supportive. But the best part for me was that I was able to pursue a passion of mine. When I was a young, single teacher, I discovered the national parks in a big way. I worked a total of five summers at three national parks—Rocky Mountain Park in Colorado, Yellowstone, and the Grand Canyon. As a result I became a hiking enthusiast. I am especially excited about chance encounters with animals while hiking. While hiking at the national parks, I encountered marmots, elk, bighorn sheep, moose, beavers, a weasel, a porcupine, two bears, and lots of deer. My animal adventures have left me with many stories to tell. My two bear encounters are both good stories, though not nearly as dangerous as you might think, fortunately. Many of my other stories are about things I have seen from the safety of an automobile. I had a large cougar run in front of my car late one night in Yellowstone. At the Grand Canyon, I had a huge owl fly directly over my little compact car, bumping its legs on my windshield, and I noticed that its wingspan was as wide as my car. Deer were, of course, plentiful in all three parks. At Grand Canyon Village, a deer would occasionally wander into the center of the village and freak out, running in panic all around. While living in Phoenix, I frequently hiked in the desert parks and the surrounding desert where I saw many roadrunners and quail, a tarantula and several rattlesnakes, including two at mountain parks in the city.

Now that I was living in rural Arizona again, I was hiking around the washes and trails in my own backyard. Here I saw one rattlesnake, a gila monster (the only one I ever saw in the wild), and a family of five javelina. The javelina growled at me, and I froze. While remaining as still as possible, I looked around with my eyes for a stick or something to use as a weapon while they continued to growl. Finally, one of the javelina broke and ran. Right after that the others followed suit, and I had another story to tell. From the window of my apartment, I often saw roadrunners and quail. I stayed at that rural school for three years. Then I was lured back to the city by the significant difference in pay. I came to regret that choice.

2008 was an eventful year politically. Barack Obama, was the first man of African descent to gain the nomination of a major political party for the US presidency. He was opposed by John McCain. McCain, a Republican from my home state of Arizona, was running with the baggage of the George Bush administration: the mistaken Iraqi War, the failure to win the Afghan War, failure to catch Osama Bin Laden, and a deep recession which hit America that year. McCain was desperate—too desperate. He chose the first term governor of Alaska, Sara Palin, as a running mate. In hindsight it appears that her only qualifications were that she was female and conservative. Now she was thrust into the national spotlight. McCain, not only lost the election, he lost the respect of many, myself included. In a worst case scenario McCain could have been elected, died, and left us President Palin—"you betcha!"[71]

I never thought that Senator McCain could redeem himself after the 2008 presidential run, but he really did. He cosponsored bipartisan immigration reform, which would have dealt humanely with long-time undocumented people and fixed much of the problem of immigration. He stood up to President Trump at a time

---

[71] Sara Palin was not the first woman nominated for the vice-presidency by a major political party. In 1984 Democrat Walter Mondale, who was running against Reagan, chose Congresswoman Geraldine Ferraro of New York for his running-mate. Ferraro received the endorsement of NOW, the National Organization of Women.

when few other Republican politicians had the courage to. Then as he was dying of brain cancer, he wrote a book promoting civil discourse. In it he admitted that his running mate selection had been a mistake without blaming her. Her selection had contributed to the coarsening of American politics.

The election of 2008 produced a Democratic majority in both houses of Congress, along with a Democratic president. The recession of 2008, the worst since the Great Depression, had created a dire economic emergency, which required an immediate response. The Obama Administration met the challenge with a stimulus package that saved the American economy, and a loan program which saved General Motors and Chrysler, facts that were soon forgotten. With lots of other challenges as yet unanswered, the Obama administration set its sights on health care reform exclusively. The idea of a comprehensive national health insurance program had been introduced by President Harry Truman in 1948 (before I was born) and had been a dream of the Democratic Party ever since. Bill and Hillary Clinton had tried and failed to deliver it in 1993. Obama saw the opening for this now. The package which was worked out was the result of much compromise. It begged fixing, but it did provide much needed relief for millions of Americans who had previously been unable to purchase affordable insurance, and it opened a door which might never be completely shut again. The current Republican push is to "repeal and replace", because repeal, by itself, is not an option now.

The Democratic Party took a hit from criticism of the Affordable Health Care Act, which Republicans quickly labeled "Obamacare," and from lack of progress in other areas, such as immigration reform and border control, and infrastructure improvements. Republicans took control of the House with the mid-term 2010 elections and gained six seats in the Senate. Republican leaders then made it known that they would not work with the President, but would do everything in their power to make certain he would not be reelected. That's how they operated, not just for the next two years, but for six years. I fault the Republican leadership, but I also fault the president for failure to woo moderate Republicans. Little progress was made with any more major legislation and the partisan political divide deepened over the next six years. This trend is showing disturbing signs of permanence today.

President Obama's foreign policy had mixed results. There were no great triumphs, but no extreme gaffs either. There was a hesitancy and unsteadiness that perhaps could be judged as overly cautious. I was disturbed by the president's tendency to speak too quickly, as when he said that Bashar Al-Assad would be gone in months, not seeming to realize that this might be interpreted as a hint about American policy. His campaign pledge to close the prison at Guantanamo on the island of Cuba was never fulfilled, though he did greatly reduce the number of detainees there. The President's biggest foreign policy success had little to do with him directly. On May 2, 2011, Navy SEALS raided a compound in Pakistan and killed Bin Laden. We later learned that Bin Laden had been living at this compound for several years within sight of a major Pakistani officer training facility.

My Republican friends were completely unrealistic in their anger and opposition to President Obama. They would say that he is "the worst president ever" which is totally ridiculous. I would get under their skins with my response, "No, he is not the worst president ever; he is not even the worst president of the twenty-first century." He even got the 2009 Nobel Peace Prize (for not being George W. Bush). And now as I write in 2018, I can say without fear of contradiction that Obama is the best president of the twenty-first century so far. I wish it were not so apparent. I interpreted the white Republican backlash against the Obama Presidency to be old fashioned, ugly racism, but in view of the current political situation, I now think that interpretation is not entirely correct. Blue collar white Americans seem to have felt abandoned by the Obama Administration and frustrated with slow economic recovery from the Great Recession despite the fact that growth was steady over eight years. The perception of abandonment may be wrong, but Democratic Party politicians need to address the perception or face the permanent defection of these former Democrats. Republicans, too, are finding that they need to pay attention to this frustrated constituency. I believe that the apparent mesmerizing appeal of Donald Trump is that blue collar Americans see him as the only politician who cares about them and, with the economy booming, blue collar Americans credit the president. I am disturbed by the president's lack of fundamental honesty and dangerous game of division. I am also concerned that the recent unfunded tax cut is a dangerous gamble unnecessary in an already booming economy designed to pander for voter approval. This tax cut is likely to burden the next generation.

I had two new television heroes during the Obama years, both were on Comedy Central. *The Daily Show* with John Stewart was fun to watch, but Stewart's prodigy, Stephen Colbert, was superb. He played a campy caricature of an extreme conservative. He also had great guests on his show and often had authors of interesting books. I miss the old Colbert Show. He is okay as the host of *Late Night* on CBS, but there is no comparison with his former show.

My radio hero was always Garrison Keillor with his *Prairie Home Companion*. He did the show for over 30 years and the show is still running on NPR, though the name of the show has been changed to *Live from Here*. I don't know how it could be the same without Keillor. I was privileged to have attended one of his live shows and one summer session special performance. The fact that Keillor later became one of the accused in the scandals of "the Me Too Movement" is heartbreaking, but I don't think that this diminishes what he had accomplish with his radio show, which brought so much joy to so many for so long.

The other classic NPR radio show which everyone loved was *Car Talk* with Tom and Ray Magliozzi, Click and Clack, two brothers who invited listeners to call in with questions about car problems. It wasn't really a motor-head program though. They told jokes, talked philosophy and culture, and had a weekly "puzzler" question. One of the brothers died of cancer recently, but because the show had run for years, NPR had years of recorded programs and continued to rerun the old episodes for over a year.

One disturbing trend that I have noticed in the twenty-first century is the senseless gun violence which shows no signs of abating. Mass-shootings were so common an occurrence during the Obama presidency that successive incidences became less and less remarkable until the Orlando nightclub massacre in which 50 were killed and another 53 injured. At that time the *Los Angeles Times* reported that between the Aurora theater shooting in 2012 and the Orlando atrocity, 218 people had been killed and 221 others injured in ten separate instances of mass-shootings in the US.[72] I was a thrilled in June 2017 to see former Arizona Congresswoman Gabrielle Giffords speak at the commissioning ceremony for the *USS Gabrielle Giffords*, after she had been shot in the head by a crazy man with a gun in a January 2011 mass-shooting in which seven were killed and thirteen injured. Though noticeably impaired, she has survived triumphantly, but even she has been unable to

---

[72] http://timelines.latimes.com/deadliest-shooting-rampages/

convince Congress to initiate any sensible gun regulation. The June 2017 attack on Republican Congressmen was a near disaster and another example of how a semi-automatic, magazine fed rifle can allow one single shooter to inflict massive casualties. The recent shootings in Las Vegas and at a Florida high school seem to be an answer to my question, *Where does it end?* It doesn't. If we talk about "gun control" the term is too vague and the argument is doomed. A better focus is on ***magazine fed weapons***, which have only two possible uses, as a toy for target practice, or as a weapon with which to commit mass murder. I'm sorry, but you should not have a Second Amendment right to a toy at the expense of those who might be murdered by such a toy. The new gun regulation movement led by the Florida students has my complete sympathy, but I don't believe it will have any lasting result. I write this hoping with all my heart that I am wrong.

Once upon a time, a majority in Congress had some courage. In 1994 Congress passed a ban on the sale of magazine fed assault weapons. Unfortunately, the law was passed with a ten year expiration date on it. By 2004 there was a serious shortage of backbone in Congress and that hasn't changed. I know that banning magazine fed weapons does little to stop gun violence in America, but the ban may have stymied one or more crazed killers. Because we can't do much to stop gun violence does not mean we should do nothing. But Congress still does not want to upset the NRA again. America's noble congressional delegates are confronted with a paradox in their profession: if they go against the NRA, they cannot be reelected; if they don't go against the NRA, they don't deserve to be reelected. But as long as they and their friends and family members aren't killed, it's probably okay to kowtow to the NRA. Courage is a virtue that Congress does not value.

9

My Engagement with the World

Another Peace Corps Adventure—Albania

I never really adjusted to teaching in the US again. Many things had changed. All the students now had cell phones, so there was always a cell phone battle, and a few students were completely addicted to their phones. I was beginning to feel pressured to do more with computers to the point where it seemed content was unimportant, as long as we did it on the computer. I do see the importance of helping the students become comfortable with computers. They live in a computer world, and education should not be different than life. Many younger teachers are able to find good, relevant material for computer assisted instruction. I was just behind the times. I could teach content very effectively, but with chalk and board and a good textbook. I am, however, unimpressed by the common core. The concept of a national curriculum seems to have merit, but I found the common core, and the extensive testing that went with it, to be stifling of real learning in both mathematics and history. I don't believe that real understanding is easily quantifiable by objective testing either, and I think that the minimal standards for all approach to education discourages challenging 75% of students. A more sensible approach would be to have three levels of achievement by which to rate the schools. For example, the goal might be for 100% of student to achieve the minimal standard, 75% of student to achieve a moderate standard, and 20% of students to achieve an advanced standard. That's a battle that the next generation of teachers will have to fight. I was suffering from boomer obsolescence, and I got out.

In 2012 I took my Arizona teacher retirement, but I did not want to take early Social Security. My solution was to flee back into the Peace Corps. This time I went alone. Karen and I had parted ways for the time being. I experienced the usual Peace Corps delays and false starts. I was first slated for Sub-Sahara Africa and I waited, then the Peace Corps developed a new site—Tunisia. My appointment was delayed. As I had experience in the Arab world, I was now assigned to this new site. I would be a part of "the Arab Spring", which had begun there, in Tunisia, and swept across the entire Arab world less than two years earlier, when a street vender burned himself to death in frustration and protest of his government. I was actually excited and looking forward to this assignment. Then about two weeks before I was scheduled to go, the American embassy in Libya was attacked, the ambassador was killed, and his body was dragged through the streets. That was too close to Tunisia. The Peace Corps cancelled the Tunisia program, and I was told that I would now be delayed until the spring. As compensation and reward for my patience, I was allowed to choose from six programs leaving that spring. I chose Albania, just north of Greece, mainly because this was a chance to see Europe. In March 2013 I was on my way to my next adventure.

Albania is located on the coast of the Adriatic Sea on the Balkan Peninsula. The word "Balkan" means mountainous and that describes Albania, but the coastline is also an attraction, and the capital, Tirana, is located in a valley. The mountains have a rugged beauty. Many of cities and villages contain charming old stone buildings, some cobblestone streets, and medieval castles. The countryside is dotted with over half a million concrete bunkers, built because the long-time communist dictator, Enver Hoxha, was paranoid about invasion. These just added to the charm for me. The whole country is an undiscovered treasure with great values for tourists. Meals and accommodations are inexpensive. The infrastructure still needs improvement, however. Roads are generally not good, uncovered holes in streets and on sidewalks are a normal hazard, power outages are not uncommon, and the wiring system in some cities is a sight to behold.

Albanians claim to have descended from the Illyrian people who were the original inhabitants of the Balkans. Their language has incorporated influence of many invading groups, but the core of the language predated all other Balkan languages and is devoid of Latin or Greek influence. Ethnic Albanians inhabit not only Albania, but also Kosovo, Montenegro, and Macedonia. Some believe that Alexander the Great was more Albanian than Greek.

Like the rest of the Balkans, Albania had been under the yoke of the Ottoman Empire for hundreds of years. A movement for independence began in the late nineteenth century when Albanian intellectuals developed an Albanian alphabet based on the Roman, not Turkish style, and began to promote the use of the Albanian language in schools. In 1912, during the second Balkan War, Albania declared independence. That independence was fragile and required the backing of the United States at the Versailles Conference after World War I. As a result, Woodrow Wilson is a hero in Albania with a statue honoring him in the capital, Tirana. Today Albania is a staunch ally of the US and a member of NATO.

Albania had an interesting history during the Cold War years. It was the last country in Eastern Europe to emerge from communism, and it is regarded to have been the most isolated and backward country in Eastern Europe at that time. Dictator Hoxha was an enthusiastic fan of Joseph Stalin, so his country was part of the original Soviet bloc, but after Stalin died the Soviet Union was no longer Stalinist enough for Enver Hoxha, so he broke off relations and defaulted on his debt to Moscow. Yugoslavia, Albania's communist neighbor to the immediate north, was also non-aligned, but the Serbs of Yugoslavia are traditional enemies of the Albanians. For a time Albania developed a relationship with Communist China, while isolating itself from all of Europe. Hoxha tried to shut down all traffic in and out of his country. The Hoxha ideal was a country completely self-contained and self-sustaining—no imports, no exports, no immigration, no emigration, no contact with the outside world. The country has been described as a giant prison with many smaller prisons within it. In a country of about three million people, there were more than 30,000 political prisoners behind bars. Television and radio broadcasts from Italy could not be blocked out, but receiving such broadcasts was illegal. People in Albania today talk about when they used to pull their curtains and watch Italian television. Apparently everyone was doing it, and almost everyone in Albania of a certain age can speak Italian. The now infamous Albanian bunkers were supposed to be a precaution in case of invasion from the US, or the Soviet Union, or Yugoslavia, or somewhere unspecified. Only in recent years has the general public in Albania become aware that Hoxha had his own personal system of elaborate, lavish, underground bunkers. These were open to the public for tours only shortly before I left the country. I never got a chance to see this personally.

Hoxha was paranoid; there was never any kind of invasion threat to him. But his resistance mentality is in keeping with Albanian history and tradition. Albania was the last place in the

Balkans to hold out against Ottoman occupation. The George Washington of Albania is Skanderbeg, an Albanian nobleman and former Ottoman military officer, who led a fifteenth century revolt against the Ottomans and held out successfully against Ottoman re-conquest. Skanderbeg's resistance is the founding legend known to all Albanians. But what happened in Albania during the World War II Nazi occupation was more remarkable to me. It is estimated that the population of Jews in Albania was only about 1,000 at the start of the German occupation, but 11,000 at the end. Jews in Albania fled to the mountains of the northeast during the war. A long-standing code of conduct practiced in that region required that any person coming to one's door requesting asylum must be granted protection. The people of the mountains stubbornly refused to turn over Jews to the occupying Nazis. When the word got out, Albania became a magnet for Jews, though getting to Albania from Central Europe during the war was difficult. In recognition of what was done then, the country of Israel later conferred upon Albania the title "Righteous Among Nations." I'm proud of my association with the good people of Albania.

The Kanun, also known as the "Code of Leke", is the code of conduct among the mountain people of Northern Albania. It was not written down, but passed orally. It governed all aspects of human relations in the Bjeshket e Nemuna, the "Accursed Mountains", of northern Albania which were untouched by government, owning to their relative inaccessibility. The sanctuary tradition exemplified the nobility of the code, but the code also has an infamous dark side. "Blood feuds" among northern clans are real and perpetual. While I was in the country, I read that it was estimated that more than 1000 men were locked up inside and did not dare go out because of blood feuds. The government has tried to intervene in recent years to end some of these feuds.

As I was preparing to go to Albania, I read *High Albania* (1909), a rather famous account of the mountain people written by Edith Durham, a British anthropologist of the Balkans who braved the wilds of the Albanian north-country in the early twentieth century.[73] Then I read *Broken April* (1978), the most famous novel by Albania's greatest novelist, Ismail Kadare. The two accounts are remarkably similar. Taken together they provide a fascinating glimpse into a medieval type society which has survived into the twenty-first

---

[73] Edith Durham must have been a remarkable woman. She travel essentially alone to the remotest parts of the Balkans.

century. Kadare has illuminated all aspects of Albanian life in various novels over his long career. He has been considered for the Nobel Prize for Literature many times, but has never received it. Many Albanians are unhappy about this. I can image a reaction of anger and disgust among my Albanian friends recently when Bob Dylan was awarded the prize.

As my group and I began to prepare for service in Albania, we were told that the country is 70% Muslim. I had a vision of a country similar to Jordan. That turned out to be far from reality. Muslim head scarfs are rare and women dress in western style. The people tend to be culturally Muslim, but few Albanians actually practice the faith. Among those who do practice it, most are of the Bektashi branch, which is very moderate. Bektashis drink alcohol, don't fast during Ramadan, and emphasize toleration of other religions and respect for Christians.

Of the non-Islamic 30% of the population, Greek Orthodox, are common in the south near the Greek border, and Roman Catholics dominate parts of the north. Italy and Greece both have had considerable influence on Albanian culture. But, unlike people in other countries, Albanians don't let religions separate them. They have a famous adage, "The religion of Albania is Albanianism." The Catholic nun, Mother Theresa, who recently became Saint Theresa, is ethnically Albanian and is a national treasure revered by all Albanians. Pope Francis actually visited the Albanian capital, Tirana, while I was there. I stood within twenty feet of him as he rode through the carefully controlled crowd at Mother Theresa Square. The crowd was large and enthusiastic. I suspect that many were Muslim or atheist, but appreciative of the honor of the Papal visit. The communist government which had controlled the country until 1992, tried to stamp out all religion. I think the long-run effect was to help dampen already weak religious passions and make people more tolerant.

My experience in Albania was fabulous. While in training, I stayed with a very nice family which had three beautiful college age daughters who were also lovely on the inside. The parents, Arif and Shpresa, were in their late 40s or early 50s, much younger than I. They were all very nice and tried hard to help me learn the language. Our training village was a picturesque setting in the mountains. This village had had large numbers of Peace Corps trainees many times before and the people were friendly and accommodating.

The most challenging thing about our training was the weather. We had arrived in the middle of March, which is the height of the rainy season. It rained almost every day. Every day was cold and damp. And Albania does not have central heating anywhere, so everywhere was cold. Our classrooms were cold and the houses we lived in were cold. The family I lived with, like many others, got through the winter by using a potbelly stove in the kitchen on which they also cooked. The result was that while the entire rest of the house was freezing cold, the kitchen was just the opposite—blazing hot. I would come into the kitchen with all my layers of clothes and almost roast.

I remember the exact date that I left my training village to assume my Peace Corps duties because it was my sixty-fourth birthday. I planned to take the first bus out with two other volunteers early that morning, which meant that I needed to get up very early. Arif insisted on knowing the exact minute I planned to get up, which I thought was a little odd. But he insisted, so I finally said, "Ok, 5:05." We had a violent thunderstorm that night. One of my prospective travelling companions called me to ask if I still intended to go. "Hell yah!" It was time to go. I was anxious to begin my real job. I set my alarm to be certain that I was up on time, and precisely at 5:05 Arif arrived at my door with a birthday cake with the number "64" and one lit candle. I ate breakfast with the family, and Arif hired a car to take me to the bus in the rain. One traveling companion met me on the bus.

I was especially anxious to get to my new home because it was in the capital city, which is really the only large city in Albania. I had been given what I think was the best volunteer job in the entire Peace Corps. Most Peace Corps volunteers go out into the countryside to serve. But because I had a Ph.D. and previous Peace Corps experience, I was sent to Tirana to work with the professional English Teachers Association, the University of Tirana, the National Library, and the British Council. I was also given a great deal of freedom to design my own program. I worked with teachers, graduate students, undergraduate students, high school students, and middle school and elementary students. I walked everywhere. Often I walked to four locations in the same day and sometimes five. I loved my work, and everyone with whom I worked was appreciative.

I was also living a good life in a large city. I lived in an area near the university called "Student City." There were stores and restaurants in the area, and many nicer restaurants nearby. There was a large, wooded park only minutes away. The American Embassy was also close. Because I was in the capital, I had some dealings with the government and with the American embassy, and would occasionally get invited to official functions. I would also get lots of visits from Peace Corps colleagues. I could see the Peace Corps headquarters from the front window of my apartment. The best thing about my life then was that I got to know so many great people of all ages.

In connection with my job I discovered MOOC (Massive Open On-line classes) and the Khan Academy. Leading universities provide MOOC classes free to anyone. Most are college level classes, but many are also geared for high school students. What MOOC means is that anyone anywhere has access to a world-class education if he/she has access to the internet. The Khan Academy offers tutoring in specific topics, mostly math, for elementary and high school students. The MOOC movement and other free educational sites like the Khan Academy represent an exciting revolution and wonderful opportunities for anyone who determines to take advantage of these.

Albania has a bad reputation for organized crime, stemming from movies as much as from reality. Living in the largest Albanian city, I encountered just enough hint of this to make my experience interesting. One man was shot dead just down the street from the Peace Corps office (and close to where I lived). I didn't see this or have a personal connection to it. I learned about this killing because all the Peace Corps volunteers were informed of it as a matter of policy. I did have two personal encounters which are memorable. I had walked to the National Library one morning, worked there for only an hour, and tried to walk home. The police would not let me take my normal route. I had to walk way around and take an extra half hour getting home. Why? A bomb had exploded in a building which I had walked past only an hour before. This was a site close to my apartment, which I continued to walk by every day. The day after the bombing, I tried to take some pictures of the site and was approached by a guy who politely told me that I would have to delete the picture immediately. I didn't protest. That was the only bombing I heard of in Tirana during my service. My other close encounter occurred when I happen upon a dead body on a Tirana street. The police were there and the body lay on the sidewalk partially covered. I don't know what happened. He could have fallen out of a window directly above where he laid, or he could have been struck by a car and moved to the sidewalk. He was certainly dead. The area was cordoned off. I had to walk out into the street to get around it. That is the total of my personal experience with outlaw Albania. I never saw a gun in Tirana, but another volunteer reported seeing a gunfight in another city. All of these events happened during my first few months of service. After this Tirana seemed rather dull by comparison for the next year and a half.

There was apparently some truth to the legend of an Albanian Mafia. I recall that there was a town in Southern Albania which was off limits for Peace Corps volunteers because it was a known haven for drug gangs. I was told the Albanian police were reluctant to go there. To be fair, the Peace Corps had about 50 volunteers in the country, and my colleagues traveled widely all over the country without reporting any problems in their travels. Apart from the few incidences which I related above, I never had any cause to feel unsafe.

I took only two short vacations while in Albania. I went to Vienna for Christmas with two Peace Corps colleagues. I'm not a big classical music fan, but I do like classical music. We attended a Mozart-Strauss concert (my two favorite classical composers) and a concert by the Vienna Boys Choir. We also toured the Habsburg Palace and outdoor Christmas markets. We stayed at a pension house I had found in *Lonely Planet-Austria*. It was perfect: in the heart of the action, near the concert hall, the main outdoor walking mall, and St. Stephen's Cathedral; and it was safe, quiet, and inexpensive. We sampled a lot of Viennese coffee and pastry at some very nice restaurants. We were fortunate to have been able to meet up with one of my colleagues from the university who had spent some time in Vienna before and knew the city. So, we also got a free personal and informative tour of the city.

I used my other vacation to visit friends in Jordan. I had to get special permission from Peace Corps Jordan to come. The country was believed to be becoming more dangerous with ISIS and the problems on the border in Syria and Iraq. About a year after this, the Peace Corps pulled out of Jordan completely. But I had specific places to go and specific people with whom I would be staying. I got permission. Two of my former Peace Corps colleagues were still in Jordan or in Jordan again. Andy had married a Jordanian girl and had two little girls and was teaching. Michael had returned to

Jordan to work for an NGO. They were both in Amman. We went out the first night I was there to the Amman bars. They knew their way around Amman; I didn't. I was a little surprised that there was an area of Amman with several western style bars, all of which were crowded and lively. The next day I took a bus to rural Jordan, the Jordan I knew. I went to see Abdullah and family. They were as gracious as ever and as happy to see me as I was to see them. I stayed there for a few days, and they provided a whole wing of the second floor for my comfort. We had a very nice visit.

As I was preparing to leave Albania, Karen came over to visit. We had remained in touch and had talked before about reconciling. We decide then to reconcile. On the way home we went to London for a week. We had been there before on a vacation during our Peace Corps service in Jordan. We really enjoyed London both times. Getting around using the underground is fast and easy. Theatre is fabulous and inexpensive. We saw four plays while in London this time: *Miss Saigon, Beatles Review, Oppenheimer,* and *The Elephant Man*. We also visited the main tourist sites again. The Imperial War Museum had a great display for World War I because the years 2014 through 2018 were the centennial years of that war. We also ventured into the Florence Nightingale Museum and found it interesting. London has become one of my favorite cities.

Home, but only Briefly

In June 2015 Karen and I came to live Flagstaff, Arizona, where I had attended graduate school. I attempted retirement. I bought a new car, a 2015 Ford Fiesta. It was my treat to myself, the first new car I had purchased in forty years. We did some traveling during that next year. We went to Las Vegas where we got remarried in the company of twenty some friends and family. My son was the best man and Karen's sister was the maid of honor again for the second time, twenty-five years later. We drove back east, visiting people along the way in South Carolina and Virginia. We visited Karen's family in upstate New York and made another trip to the Baseball Hall of Fame in Cooperstown where I linger and read, recalled and reflected on the magic of baseball. On the way back, we stopped in Michigan to visit friends with whom we had taught on the Navajo Reservation all those years ago. We visited my cousins in Wisconsin. We took care of all the visiting for a while.

In Flagstaff I tried to figure out what a retired life should be. I volunteered at a charity thrift store and tutored with Literacy Volunteers. From that I was able to get on with the local community college as a paid tutor. The paid work was validation that I had something of value to contribute. I admit that I needed that feeling. I also was able to find a math tutoring job at a local charter elementary school. This was also important validation for me. I joined Toastmasters briefly. And I signed Karen and me up for "Friends of Flagstaff", an organization which matches local people up with foreign university students who are new to the area. We were matched with two Chinese students, nice young men with whom we are still in contact. I also got season tickets to the university football games. Northern Arizona University plays in the Big Sky Conference, NCAA Division 1 Football Championship Subdivision (formerly Division 1-AA) and is competitive at that level. They also play in a domed stadium, which is always comfortable. The games are fast and exciting on the AstroTurf. Scores are often high, as Big Sky defenses seem generally to be shaky. The games are great fun.

Flagstaff is a highly desirable location for outdoor enthusiasts and hikers like me. It is only 70 miles from the Grand Canyon and less than 30 miles from Sedona, which may be the most beautiful place in the United States. The city of Flagstaff is at an elevation of 7000 feet which means that it gets lots of snow. A well-known ski resort is located just outside of town on Mount Humphreys, at 12,000 feet, the highest peak in Arizona. The mountain affords a challenging and invigorating hike in the summer. Other wonderfully interesting and challenging hikes are within an hour's drive. Hiking the Grand Canyon requires stamina, but the beauty and mystery of the hike is worth the effort. Hiking to the bottom and back out in the same day is discouraged by the park rangers, but it's a fun physical challenge for those who are up to it. The drive from Flagstaff to Sedona goes through Oak Creek Canyon, which is beautiful in and of itself. Shortly after passing Slide Rock State Park, an idyllic natural water park frequented by large numbers of NAU students, one emerges into the red rock country of Sedona. Sedona is a feast for the eyes. Many "New Age" enthusiasts also claim that the region contains vortexes which produce psychic energy. Flagstaff, itself is surrounded by forest. This area used to be part of the largest continuous stand of Ponderosa Pine in the world, until it was devastated by wildfires, which have been plaguing the west in recent years, as the region becomes hotter and drier.

Another Foreign Adventure—Vietnam

I really tried to be retired, but after a year I was ready to try something else. Prospects in the US didn't look all that good, and I wasn't thrilled with the idea of going back into a US classroom and dealing with typical high school behavioral problems in the US, nor was I thrilled about the common core. I started to look overseas and was met with lots of interest. I soon had interviews with several enthusiastic prospective employers. My age, however, became a problem. I found that many countries do not want to grant a work visa to an older worker. The placement service I was using connected me with a school in Vietnam. I had not really considered anywhere in East Asia, but I was presented with an offer. Why not? I had missed the all-expenses paid trip that my government had been providing to young men in the 1960s and 70s.

The school was in Ho Chi Minh City, the former Saigon. I was assigned to teach math, history, and English. The organizations leaders also wanted me to be the vice-principal. They were very insistent upon that, but I was just as resistant. The year started off well. The students were respectful, though not always attentive. I had to train them to not engage in conversations while I was teaching and to put their phones away. I never really quite won the phone battle with some of them. Vietnamese kids are not all that different from American kids.

We had started the year with all faculty positions filled, but with an acting-principal on loan from the university which was part of the same organization. Soon a principal was hired and a teacher was fired. My workload and the workloads of others were expanded to take up the slack for the fired teacher. During this time I was teaching from 8 AM until 4:45 PM solid, except for an hour lunch break. I had no preparation time and five different lessons to prepare every day. I found it impossible to deliver the same quality lessons I had been delivering, and I was busy every night with grading and preparations. I was overjoyed when a replacement teacher was hired.

All went along well until the middle of November when I was called into the office and informed of another personnel change. The principal had resigned suddenly, and I would be the new principal. I had no training, experience, or inclination for the job. But I did have the magic letters, P-H-D. The same magic letters that landed me the cushy Peace Corps assignment in Albania now landed me in hot water, over my head. I protested and the organizational leadership insisted. So, I became a principal. It was an entertaining position. I also continued to teach three periods a day that first year. I survived with no major gaffs, but I am ill-suited to be an administrator. I don't have the temperament for it. I don't like conflict. Karen and I enjoyed the experience the first year. I returned for a second year and a transfer to Da Nang, on the coast of central Vietnam. I wanted to return to teaching, but I was offered another substantial raise to be the principal there. I came to regret accepting the offer and consequently stayed for only one more semester.

I hadn't really come to Vietnam to work. I came to explore. HCMC is a city of about 8.5 million people and 4 million motorbikes. Traffic jams with hundreds of motorbikes are the norm on major streets. For those of us less daring, there is a reliable, inexpensive bus system. Old Saigon is only a small part of the city today, but many people and businesses still use the name Saigon. The city features many high-rise buildings today and construction is progressing rapidly all over. We lived in a high-rise hotel. The central city, old Saigon, caters to western tourists. It has many American, Italian, Mexican, and other ethnic restaurants. It also has shopping malls, an opera house, and a good (Vietnam War) war museum. Many American Vietnam War veterans return as tourists to their Saigon and they are welcomed wholeheartedly. For 25 cents I could ride the bus from my house to the city center in 25 minutes or less. I walked there once just to see if I could do it. It took about an hour.

The War Museum is discomforting for me as an American, but also important, and doubly so for me as a historian. It is obviously dedicated to showing the communist side of the war story. However, one floor is entitled "Just the Facts" and it is surprisingly what it claims to be, though it may not be all the facts. These exhibits do not hide the fact that there was a significant resistance to the communists among the people of the south.

The museum also has a section on "American War Crimes". What is missing to provide balance is anything about communist war crimes. Nevertheless, all Americans should know about the My Lai Massacre and about Agent Orange. As I have previously mentioned, I do not believe that it was ever realistic to think that a chemical agent which kills plants would not also be toxic to people and animals. Or were American leaders aware of what they were doing but not caring? Most Vietnamese with whom I came in contact either didn't remember or didn't want to remember anything about the war. Of course, no one under the age of 45 has any personal memory of the war. But some who do care would like America to own responsibility for what was done. The War Museum display claims that three million Vietnamese still suffer from effects of Agent Orange.

While the US lost that war, most American war aims seem to have been realized. US-Vietnamese trade was booming when I was living in Vietnam. Vietnam is still officially a communist country—one of only five remaining in the world. But as I have seen it, the economic system of the country is strongly capitalist. The communist government's only apparent involvement is with too many awkward regulations and what appears to be corrupt licensing practices. "The Colonel" has led a new, more successful American invasion of Vietnam. KFC is everywhere in the cities; McDonalds can be easily found in Ho Chi Minh City and Hanoi; Baskin Robbins and Burger King also have a strong presence. And I have seen Pizza Hut and Subway.

There seems also of be a fair amount of freedom of expression in the society—I would say much more so than in some US allied nations. The American school at which I worked did have some restrictions, but the mechanism for enforcement was weak. The American University in Vietnam, which my company opened in August 2016, is an example of the openness. American business and management ideas seem to be welcome. And I heard an interesting statistic on NPR recently. A 2016 survey found that 80% of Vietnamese have a favorable opinion of the United States. This verifies what I have experienced personally. The funny thing is that I don't think that 80% of Americans have a favorable opinion of America.

The domino theory had propelled the US into the Vietnam War. So was the theory valid in East Asia? The first country of the region to become communist was North Korea. Communists were invited in there as inducement for the USSR to join the war effort against Japan. Then in 1949 the Chinese communists emerged victorious in their long struggle. This was the event which shocked the west and led to increased fear that the former French colony of Indochina was vulnerable. Laos, Cambodia, and Vietnam had all been under military occupation by Japan as French Vichy territories during World War II. The French were attempting to reestablish control after the war with some resistance. Laotian and Vietnamese leaders had declared independence in 1945. The French agreed to autonomy for Laos in 1949 and complete independence for that country in 1953 as a constitutional monarchy. What followed in Laos was a civil war between monarchists and communists. That civil war continued until 1975 and became part of the larger US-Vietnam War with the US bombing communists in Laos, and North Vietnamese forces invading to support the communist side. The Vietnamese leader who had declared independence was the communist, Ho Chi Minh. He fought the French until 1954 then agreed to a temporary division of the country at the 17th parallel until 1956. When the government of the "democratic South" refused to hold elections to reunify the country, as had been agreed upon, North Vietnam invaded the south and the US-Vietnam War began. The third Indochina country, Cambodia, appeared to offer no threat, having been allowed independence from France in 1953 as a monarchy. But it was also dragged into the Vietnam War because the Vietcong were using it as a safe haven for raids into South Vietnam. This precipitated an American incursion, which provoked a communist revolution that deposed the king. The communist Pol Pot seized dictatorial power and had millions of his own people killed as he attempted to move people out of the cities onto collective farms. The film *The Killing Field* is a dramatization of this period.[74]

What the people of Indochina wanted was independence. What the US and other western democracies feared was that the communist doctrine of shared wealth would have great appeal in Indochina after the experience of colonial exploitation in which a few foreigners became wealthy by the labor of masses of peasants. If all of Indochina became communist, the people of the Indian sub-continent would be encouraged to become communist as they also struggled with the problems of emerging from colonial rule. Other peoples in Malaysia, Indonesia, and Africa would also see advantages in communism. If this chain of events occurred, then the socialist movement in Europe would be reignited.

Proponents of the domino theory made the assumption that newly emerging communist countries would join the Soviet (Russian) bloc, forming a military alliance, which would threaten western democracies, and a trading alliance, which might eventually isolate a few remaining capitalist democracies. The Soviet communist government of that time was dictatorial and savagely suppressive

---

[74] *The Killing Fields*, David Puttnam producer, Goldcrest Films, 1984.

of human rights while failing to deliver a reasonable standard of living. While Soviet communism claimed to be the antithesis of fascism, it had proven to be its darker mirror image. The dystopian end of this communist wave would, it was feared, be a world in which a few elites controlled the masses with thought control, the absence of liberty, and brutality for anyone who would resist. If this sounds ridiculous today, we should recall that this was the reality for decades in the Soviet Union, China, and North Korea, and with a tight mechanism of suppression in place, it was believed that countries becoming communist would be lost forever.

But the communization of French Indochina did not appear to have much effect on the remainder of South Asia. Also, communism did not prove to be monolithic. By the late 1960s a rift between Soviet Russia and Communist China was already noticeable. Shortly after its victory over the Americans and the southern nationalists in 1975, the communist government of Vietnam waged two more wars, both against other communist countries—China and Cambodia. We know now that solidarity among communist countries was only a twentieth century concept, but enmity between Vietnam and China is historically enduring. China has considered Vietnam as a subordinate, vassal state for centuries, and the Vietnamese have always resented Chinese arrogance. China and Vietnam are still not on good terms today, as China looks to dominate trade and navigation in the South China Sea. (Vietnamese prefer to call it the East Sea.) Vietnam also invaded the newly established communist Cambodia in 1978 and overthrew the dictator, Pol Pot, whose regime of terror did not discriminate between native Cambodians and Vietnamese nationals. The royal family of Cambodia was restored to the throne.

There are only five countries left in the world which still claim to be communist today. Four are in East Asia—China, North Korea, Laos, and Vietnam. The fifth communist country is Cuba. Communism failed in the Soviet Union, Eastern Europe, Nicaragua, and Cambodia. Transition to democratic capitalism was relatively peaceful in all of these except Cambodia. China and Vietnam are moving rapidly toward greater capitalism, and Vietnam is moving slowly toward more openness. Vietnam has become an important trade partner of the United States and a wary adversary of China. North Korea is a dangerous, backward, one man dictatorship with a depressed standard of living. Cuba is showing signs of emerging into the larger world with budding capitalistic tendencies. It is fair to say that democratic capitalism is winning spectacularly over autocratic socialism worldwide. Capitalism has finally been shown to clearly deliver a better standard of living than socialism, but democratic capitalism has also shown itself to benefit from socialist modifications; in America these include Social Security, Medicare, Medicaid, and Obamacare. Freedom of thought and expression will continue to gain in the twenty-first century as the internet now makes suppression of ideas more and more difficult. Totalitarianism and one-party rule are on the wrong side of history and cannot last without severe repression.

My experience in Vietnam did change my view of the war slightly. I got the impression from what I saw that there was significant anticommunist feeling in the larger cities of the south, Saigon and Da Nang, and among some ethnic minority groups. Even the National War Museum confirms this opinion. The US did have a commitment to these people. So, the option of just pulling out abruptly would have appeared to be a cruel trick on legitimate allies. But my impression of the general will of the country was not changed. I still think that most of the rural people were either pro-communist or apathetic. The capitalist system did not offer them any great benefit, and the US military was either dismissive or deadly hostile when encountering rural people.

Asian Travels

Explorations we did while living in Vietnam were pleasurable. We cruised the Mekong Delta and took small boats between the islands. We went to Cambodia for a week at Christmas to explore the ancient Buddhist temples of Angkor Wat. The *Laura Croft, Tomb Raider* movies with Angelina Jolie were made there. The temples are truly impressive and otherworldly appearing. While exploring them we stayed in Siem Reap which is worth visiting by itself, because the whole town caters to western tourists. The main street is Pub Street. It's brightly lit and lively at night. I have observed that Asians love glitzy lights. Another interesting thing about Siem Reap is that all our financial transactions were done in US dollars. Even when I went to the ATM for cash, it spit out US dollars.

We made three trips to Da Nang the first year, before my transfer to be the principal of the school there in my second year. Da Nang is right on the coast. It's a tourist attraction and an attraction for a significant expatriot community with lots of glitz and bright lights at night. It was the site of a large US airbase during the US-Vietnam War. It had also been the center of the Cham civilization in ancient and medieval times. The city's museum of Cham sculptures is impressive. There are also ancient pagodas and an Asian theme park. A river runs mostly parallel to the ocean through the city. Cruises on the river are a popular tourist activity, and the main bridge over the river has the image of a dragon in lights which changes color from green to yellow at night. On weekends the dragon breathes fire. The mountains, an hour's drive away, have a very long cable car to the top which has a Disneyseque theme park.

Our last Vietnam adventure was an excursion to Hanoi and Ha Long Bay. I had been reluctant to go to Hanoi, not knowing how Americans would be received there, but friends who had been there assured me that Americans are welcome and encouraged me to make the trip. I'm glad that I did. Hanoi is different from Saigon. The communist presence is more open, but western tourists are everywhere and welcomed. The old city has lots of narrow, interesting streets to explore. American and western restaurants are common. A small lake on the edge of the old city is the social center for tourists. It features street performers, snack food, entertainment for kids, and wide walkways for a leisurely stroll around the lake. We stayed in a nice hotel right in the old city. The service in the hotel was terrific, breakfasts were great, and at a price of only $70 per night. Our Ha Long Bay cruise was also delightful. Ha Long Bay is a world heritage site at the south end of the famous Gulf of Tonkin. Some of the 2017 film *King Kong Skull Island* was filmed there. There are hundreds of islands in the bay and one very large cave on one of the islands.

The one big vacation we took while in Vietnam was to Western Australia. I didn't want to go the Sydney, because it was a longer trip, and the west coast of Australia was long enough. That west coast turned out to be a perfect experience for what I wanted. We got a hotel right across the road from the ocean. We were half way between the city of Perth, the only large city in the west, and the port of Freemantle, a picturesque seaside town which once had been the main port for that part of the country. Out a short distance in the ocean is the island of Rottnest which had been used as a prison for aboriginal convicts in the nineteenth century and is now an attraction for snorkelers. We toured the prison and took photos of the quokkas, the odd rat-like animals for which the island is named. We shopped in Perth. We dined in Freemantle. And we laid on the beach by our hotel in Cottesloe. When I had to return to Vietnam to work, I was well rested and ready.

By pure coincidence, we were in Australia for "Australia Day", the big national holiday which commemorates when British ships first arrive on the continent. Interestingly, but not surprisingly, the indigenous Australians have a negative feeling about the day in the same way that indigenous Americans have a negative feeling toward Columbus Day.

10

American Hegemony in the New Millennium

In the first decade of this new millennium America had a well-established hegemony in the world. I will discuss the problems America has been facing since then and the erosion of some of that status. But before that, let's look at some of the most important people involved in leading the American society and the world at the turn of the millennium. I would like to suggest my list of the icons of this time which can inspire others to reignite the light of American hegemony--Bill Gates, Steve Jobs, Oprah Winfrey, Stephen Spielberg, Mark Zuckerberg, and Ellen DeGeneres. Some were born with clear advantages; Oprah was just as clearly disadvantaged. All these people achieved greatness by determination and hard work, seizing the advantages which presented themselves.

Hegemony is a position of leadership or dominance by one country or society. It is not achieved by having the strongest military or the most wealth. The people around the world follow because they want to. Hegemony is achieved through innovation, creativity, and ideas which matter. American hegemony thus far in the twenty-first century has resulted from innovations in computer technology and use, dominance in the entertainment industry, philanthropy on a scale never before seen, and ideas about a more just and more humane world. The world follows because the bright light of America is showing a better way.

Bill Gates (1955-present), Changing the World

Bill Gates was born in Seattle, Washington to an upper middle class family. His father was a lawyer and his mother was on the board of directors of the First Interstate Bank System and the United Way. He went to a private school where he had access to computers at a time when most students did not. He was even excused from math class to work on computer programming. However, Gates did not have unlimited access to computer time, as we do today. In fact, one summer he and three friends were banned from access to computers at a local center for hacking the system in order to get extra computer time. After the ban, the four boys were hired by that center to find bugs and improve the system.

Gates had written several commercial programs before his high school graduation. He graduated from high school in 1973 as a National Merit Scholar.[75] After his high school graduation he worked briefly as a page in the US House of Representatives before beginning college. He attended Harvard for two years during which he continued to work on computer programming. A project with Honeywell Corporation induced him to drop out of Harvard and establish Microsoft.

On New Year's Day 1994 Bill married Melinda French. Melinda had been the valedictorian of her high school class. She has a master's degree from Duke University. She was employed as a product developer with Microsoft at the time couple met. The couple's wealth continued to grow. Bill Gates would become the richest man in the world.

Both Bill and Melinda Gates started life with considerable advantages. To their credit they both worked hard to develop their own skills, and they recognized that those who have achieved much have a responsibility to give back to the world for all that was given to them. In 2000 they established the Bill and Melinda Gates Foundation to oversee donations to philanthropic agencies and projects. This foundation is the wealthiest philanthropic institution ever in all human history. The Gates have stated that their goal is to give away 95% of their wealth to causes which will benefit humanity. The Foundation has already had a major impact on health projects in Africa. The Gates have focused the Foundation on four world development needs. These are: health, education (especially for girls), agricultural improvement, and institutional lending to small entrepreneurs.

---

[75] Gates scored 1590 out of a possible 1600 on his SAT test. One does not score this high without serious study and preparation.

Steve Jobs (1955-2011), Inventing and Re-inventing the Apple

Steve Jobs did not know his biological parents well. He was adopted at birth in San Francisco, California. His biological father was a graduate student from Syria while his biological mother was a professor at the University of Wisconsin. Neither of Steve's adopted parents had attended college. Steve's adopted father had not even graduated from high school and worked as a "repo man".

In 1972 Steve Jobs graduated from high school and began college at Reed College in Oregon. He soon dropped out to take a job at Atari, the computer game company, joining his older boyhood friend, Steve Wozniak, who redesigned the "Pong" and "Breakout" video games for Atari. Wozniak also designed the first Apple Computer. Wozniak, Jobs, and another friend formed the Apple Computer Company in 1976.

The first Apple Macintosh computer was introduced in 1984. John Sculley had become CEO of Apple the previous year. Sculley fell into conflict with Jobs when sales of the Macintosh were less than expected. Sculley reorganized Apple in 1985, and Jobs resigned from the company at that point. After leaving Apple, Jobs first founded the NeXT computer company. Then he invested in Pixar, the company which would lead the way in full length, animated films, partnering with Disney Studios. Jobs eventually sold his Pixar shares to Disney and took a seat on the board of directors of Disney.

In 1997 Apple purchased NeXT Computers and rehired Jobs as CEO. Apple was struggling at the time. Under Jobs' new leadership Apple introduced the iPod, iPhone, and iPad. Apple went from near extinction to a position of dominance in the market again because Jobs designed truly innovative products for which there was no demand until after the product was on the market. Then Jobs had to convince consumers that they needed these products. This is a bold strategy, which no one seemed to have previously considered. Today Apple Computers is the wealthiest corporation in America.

Oprah Winfrey (1954-present), O! Oprah!

O! Oprah has a truly inspirational life story. She was born in poverty to a single, teenage mother in rural Mississippi in 1954. Oprah was sexually molested at 9, and pregnant at 14. But she had grit. During high school in Nashville, Tennessee, Oprah Winfrey was an honor student, member of the speech team, and voted "Most Popular Girl." At age 17 she won the Miss Black Tennessee beauty contest and got a job as a radio news announcer while in high school. At the age of 19, Winfrey was reporting television news and hosting a talk show in Chicago, Illinois. She went to college on a full scholarship and studied journalism.

After college she worked as a television news anchor in Nashville, Tennessee and Baltimore, Maryland before co-hosting a talk show in Baltimore in 1978. She later hosted a second morning talk show in Chicago, Illinois. A sharp mind and an intense interest in social justice made her talk shows compelling. From 1986 through 2001, Oprah's talk show was nationally televised and hugely popular. She elevated the topics and discussion with the goal of contributing something of value to the lives of her viewers. Her show was watched all over the world and she had a significant impact on thought everywhere. She offered a first class intellect and a woman's perspective which could not be ignored. She is proud of her African-American heritage but not limited by it. It only adds another layer of richness to her. I know from my personal experience that women in Jordan still felt inspired by her and connected to her when I was in that country in 2005-2007. Oprah is a world phenomenon.

Oprah retired from her show while it was still immensely popular. She wanted to expand her horizons into other fields. She co-founded the women's cable television network, Oxygen, her own television production company, Harpo Productions, and her own magazine, *O Magazine*. All three of these endeavors have been successful. And she has co-authored 5 books.

Lady O. has also been acclaimed as an actress. In 1985 she was featured in the much-admired movie, *The Color Purple*, and was nominated for an Academy Award. In 1998 Winfrey produced and starred in *Beloved*, a film adaptation of Toni Morrison's Pulitzer Prize winning novel. Oprah has also acted in many other movies. In 2018 she became the first African-American woman to receive the Cecil B. DeMille Lifetime Achievement Golden Globe Award.

Today Ms. Winfrey is among the richest people in the world and is also considered to be one of the most influential throughout the world. She has honorary doctoral degrees from Harvard and Duke. She was awarded the Presidential Medal of Freedom in 2013. And she is among the world's leading philanthropists. She has given away hundreds of millions of dollars to a variety of causes. Winfrey is so well know that she is known instantly by her first name, Oprah. Having faced down all challenges while uplifting people everywhere, Oprah says, "Excellence is the best deterrent to racism or sexism."

Stephen Spielberg (1946-present) and American Films

Stephen Spielberg was born to an orthodox Jewish family in Cincinnati, Ohio. Before Stephen finished school the family moved first to New Jersey, then to Phoenix, Arizona, then to Saratoga, California. As a small child Stephen experienced bullying, often related to antisemitism. He started making amateur films at the age of 12. At the age of 13, Spielberg won a prize for a 40 minute film he produced using classmates as actors. At 16 he produced his first full length motion picture for $500. He was also a serious Boy Scout. He achieved the highest scout rank, eagle scout. Stephen's parents divorced shortly before he finished high school.

Spielberg attended California State University-Long Beach briefly. While there, he served an internship with Universal Studios. As an intern he was given the opportunity to produce a short film which so impressed of studio executives that he was offered a seven year contract to produce films for Universal. Spielberg's first big directorial success was *Jaws*. The movie made him famous and a millionaire. *Close Encounters of the Third Kind* followed, written and directed by Spielberg. Famous Spielberg films are many. They include the *Indiana Jones* movies; *Saving Private Ryan; Schindler's List; E.T., the Extra-terrestrial; The Color Purple; Empire of the Sun; Jurassic Park; Gremlins; Poltergeist;* and *Amistad*.

Amistad and later Spielberg films are a testament to the power of film to educate and inspire while entertaining. His crowning achievements thus far are the historical films *Schlinder's List* and *Saving Private Ryan*. Both of these films won him Academy Awards for best director. In 1994 Stephen Spielberg co-founded DreamWorks Pictures. The following year Spielberg was awarded the American Film Institute's Lifetime Achievement Award. The movies have made Spielberg a billionaire, and Spielberg films have helped to cement Hollywood's leadership in the film industry. American film continues to project an image of America admired by the world. And Spielberg has proven that film, at its best, can inspire a better world.

Mark Zuckerberg (1984-present), the Face of Social Media

Mark Zuckerberg was the leading co-founder of Facebook. He is the current CEO and board chairman. Zuckerberg attended college preparatory high schools. He was an excellent student with special interest in languages, sciences, and computers. He took advanced college classes in computer programming while in high school. He was also captain of the fencing team.

Zuckerberg created Facebook for Harvard students while a student there. The growth and success of Facebook led him to drop out of Harvard. The number of people with Facebook accounts today is approximately 2 billion. (There are only 8 billion people in the world.) On December 9, 2010, Zuckerberg, Bill Gates, and Warren Buffett signed a promise they called "The Giving Pledge", by which they each promised to donate to charity at least half of their wealth and challenged all other super-wealthy people to do the same. Zuckerberg's charitable donations up to now have totaled approximately $1 billion.

Facebook, however, is not without controversy. Use of Facebook is an obsession for many young people to the point of addiction. Recently, there have been charges that Facebook has been used by foreign countries to manipulate the 2016 US presidential election. And Facebook has been accused of sharing too much of its users private data with third parties. Yet after all, Facebook is undeniably a major contributor to the dominance of American culture and thought in the twenty-first century. And the philanthropic foundation Zuckerberg establish with his wife Pricilla Chen is working to "advance human potential and promote equality in areas such as health, education, scientific research and energy"[76] with well-funded projects to promote communities of scientists, physicians, engineers, and teachers.

Ellen DeGeneres (1958-present), More than OK

Ellen DeGeneres is probably the least internationally known of the icons on my list, though she is very popular in the US with a nationally televised show which continues to have a strong following.

---

[76] https://www.chanzuckerberg.com/initiatives

She attended the University of New Orleans for one semester in 1976. She began doing stand-up comedy at clubs in New Orleans in 1981. She continued to do stand-up comedy on tour during the 1980s. Her big break was her first appearance on *The Tonight Show with Johnny Carson* in 1986. She eventually got her own television show, the popular situation comedy *Ellen* from 1994 through 1998.

In an act of courage which was to be revolutionary at the time, DeGeneres announced to the world that she is gay (homosexual) on the *Oprah Winfrey Show* in 1997. Shortly after that, her character "Ellen" in her sitcom discussed her sexual orientation with a psychiatrist played by Winfrey. The admission and embrace of her sexual orientation openly was a brave and pioneering move at that time. The larger message is that it is okay. Sexual orientation is part of who we are, but who we are is much bigger; and sexual orientation is a personal thing—one's own business. DeGeneres's simple message of humanity is still inspiring in America and revolutionary in many parts of the world.

Since 2003 Ellen DeGeneres has been hosting her popular talk show. It is a celebration of humanity and women's empowerment and uplifting in the style of the Oprah Winfrey model. She has hosted the Oscars (films), the Grammys (music), and the Day Time Emmys (television). She is the author of three books and the founder of her own record company which gives a voice to lesser known artists. She has won 13 Emmys and 14 Peoples' Choice Awards.

True Achievement

The American leaders discussed in this chapter all unquestionably achieved greatness by what they added to the world—products, which have contributed to wealth and well-being; thought, which continues to move society to greater humanity; and philanthropy which is uplifting millions throughout the world.[77] This is what has created American hegemony.

---

[77] Four of these six people are "baby boomers"—Gates, Jobs, Spielberg, and Winfrey.

Major Cultural Events of the Third Millennium

(2000) This is actually the last year of the second millennium.	Bill and Melinda Gates establish the Bill and Melinda Gates Foundation.	This is the richest philanthropic organization in the history of the world, and it is big enough to be making a noticeable impact over the entire world.
2010	Mark Zuckerberg founds Facebook.	
2012	John Green publishes *The Fault is in Our Stars*.	Green's work inspires pre-teens to read, to appreciate literature, and to care about others.
2016	Jamaican sprinter Usain "Lighting" Bolt, the world's fastest man, wins three Gold Medals in the 2016 Olympics. This was his third straight Olympics with Gold Medals in the 100, 200, and share of the 4 x 400 meter races.	
2016	American swimmer Michel Phelps appears in his fourth straight Olympics and extends his record of Gold Medals and total medals. He is the most decorated Olympian of modern times.	
2017	1976 Olympic decathlon Gold Medal winner Bruce Jenner has a sex change and becomes Caitlyn Jenner.	

11

Problems of the Twenty-first Century and Conclusions

We used to think that the greatest threat to America this century is terrorism. Maybe it was at the beginning of the century. But today access to information is the problem. While there is much more information available than ever before in history, it's also organized in such a way that one can choose the news to support whatever biases, prejudices, or other misconception he holds, and no one needs to be exposed to ideas which are challenging. Conservatives watch FOX News. MSNBC provides the opposite alternative on the left, though it does not command as large an audience. I can watch FOX News and I could even listen to Bill O'Reilly when he was there, though I disagree with the slant. Unfortunately, many people watch FOX News thinking that they are getting the objective truth, and some won't watch any other news because only FOX has the truth. Slack on the left is taken up by the late night television hosts Stephen Colbert, Seth Meyers, Trevor Noah, and Samantha Bee. Even though I may agree with these laugh-seekers, I still find it unfortunate that for some people, they provide a principle source of news.

While FOX News and late night talk shows attempt to divide us, commercial talk radio is a bigger threat to democracy. The talk radio personalities tend to have extreme views because audiences seem to prefer this. Many of these radio personalities also seem to be poorly informed themselves and lacking in real credibility. Extremist radio hosts validate the extreme views of the listeners. I have actually tried to listen to Rush Limbaugh on at least two occasions. But both times he expressed such ugly, personal attacks that I was too disgusted to listen more than five minutes, and he offered no substantive discussion of any real issues. Yet Rush is a hero to millions. The right wing radio personalities are selling fear and greed, and these things are driving much of our politics.

Television is divisive, radio is divisive, and now the internet is hopelessly divisive. With most Americans on Facebook, we are bombarded with ideas with which we agree, and in constant contact with others with whom we agree. We surf the net for information about the causes we care about, and the internet responds by feeding us other sites for the things we have sought. We search for groups with which we agree, and the net continues to send us information from other groups with which we agree.

Our World Wide Web is creating extremes, and education is failing to rise to the challenge. The situation is moving in a disturbing direction.

Divisiveness is one of two intrinsic problems that the internet presents which are historic in the twenty-first century. The other, equally troubling related problem is an explosion of un-vetted information. Before the internet, news stories could only get widespread circulation by propagation through some large scale news agency. Any large-scale news agency has its credibility as an essential resource which must always be carefully guarded. These news agencies continue to vet stories with care to protect their reputations, but today many people get information from the net without considering the source because it happens to be in print, maybe very authentic looking. The problem cries out for educating people about evaluating information. The challenge is great and schools do not appear be up to this challenge. In the meantime we have millions of adults who are not able to distinguish truth from fiction, and probably will never be able to—and they vote—and they own guns.

Polarization is a major problem extending into our government because those whom we elect to govern allow it to be. While both major parties in Congress fail to do the country's business, I must give the Republicans credit for honesty. The Democrats promise everything and do nothing, but the Republicans promise nothing and do exactly that. A striking disconnect exists between the very low approval rating of Congress, which exists today because of its inability to get things done, and the fact that most people approve of their individual members of Congress. All those good members of Congress whom we elect cannot do their jobs because they have a distorted sense of priorities related to who they are. No one is elected to represent the Democrats among his constituency, nor is anyone elected to represent the Republicans. They are all elected to do the country's business. The real thinking members of Congress are not extremists; they are moderates. Left to their own preferences, moderate Republicans and moderate Democrats could work together to craft the best compromises to move the country forward. But the parties enforce party loyalty. The Congressman who is not loyal to the party will not get appointments to important, prestigious committees whereby he/she can build a reputation for leadership without really leading at all. Ironically, though most politicians deplore divided government (congressional majority of one party and president of the other party), divided government has proven to be more efficient than single party rule, because, with divided government, the parties are forced to work together. Prominent examples of successful divided governments are Eisenhower and Reagan with the Democrats, and Clinton with the Republicans.

The parties, BOTH parties, need reforming. As radical polarization in both parties has driven moderates out, the parties are becoming more incapable of doing the country's business, though they still maintaining control of the political machinery. An ever growing number of Americans are registering to vote as "independents". We want to applaud the idea of "independent" minded voters, but the fact is that by registering as "independent", good, thinking people somewhat restrict their own voices, which are desperately needed. If you are an independent, please join a party! I don't care if you join the Democratic Party or the Republican Party. Pick one and use your voice to make that party better. Then vote independently.

Let's Reason Together

Americans need to learn to reason together, rather than allow politicians to divide us to serve only their narrow self-interests. I lament that our education system is unable to produce thoughtful citizens who can sift through the barrage of information and make informed decisions. I actually saw disturbing signs of things to come long ago while I was teaching. We have a tendency to relish debate as a form of verbal combat. Winning is more important than arriving at an intelligent conclusion. We do need to train lawyers. Lawyers are important to the functioning of the legal system, but most people will not be trial lawyers. We really need to train citizens to speak to each other thoughtfully and respectfully. I tell you what my concerns are, and you tell me yours. We both make an effort to understand each other and come to a solution which meets everyone's needs without emotional involvement. This is not easy to do. We all tend to become emotional when talking about those issues which stir our passions. Emotional involvement leads to hardening of our positions and defensive attitudes which block compromise. We all need to get past this barrier by acknowledging the reasons for the emotions of the other, while we each keep our own emotions in check. Compromise between honest, well-meaning people is needed to continue to move society forward.

Another human tendency, which we also need to counter, is the natural inclination to disagree with everything an opponent says simply because we know that we have fundament disagreements. In fact, no one is wrong 100% of the time, and not even the brightest person is correct 100% of the time. I would like to suggest this exercise to promote healthy discussion: Consider carefully the pronouncements of the politicians with whom you most disagree. Find three to five of this person's statements with which you agree. Then do the same for a politician with whom you most agree, but now find an equal number of this person's positions with which you disagree. The purpose of the exercise is to get each person to think beyond one destructive shortcut we often take.

Personally, I am for gay rights because all people are equal, but I can understand why committed Christians might oppose gay marriage. I am in favor of legal ownership of hand guns, hunting rifles, and even shotguns with proper vetting of all purchasers, but I don't want anyone to have a military style assault rifle. I also believe that failure to secure one's weapons which are consequently used in a felony crime should itself be a felony crime. I favor "choice" because I think a woman should have dominion over her own body, but I respect the right of "pro-life" supporters to argue respectfully against abortion. I don't believe that nudity is obscene, but prejudicial hate speech is. I think everyone should know the truth of the Holocaust, but no one should feel entitled because of it. I believe in justice and mercy, but I don't believe in legal loopholes for the guilty. I think that the border wall the president is proposing should be built because the majority of Americans want it, but with the provision that funding will be contingent on immigration reform that includes a path to citizenship for undocumented people in the US who have no other criminal record and pay a fine ($1000 per person perhaps) for breaking the immigration law. Yes, let's close off the illegal immigration through Mexico, but let's have a free trade agreement because it's good for all of North America. I would also add that programs to help development in Mexico and Central

America would also be desirable. I know that few people will agree with me on every issue, but I see value in people of goodwill coming together to compromise for the common good.

The Power of Advertising

Unfortunately, in America's mass society, mass advertising appears to be able to get many people to believe anything. Large scale advocacy groups backed by massive funding are often successful at framing a message in a way that people think that what is good for that group is also good for everyone else and morality is not an issue. For this, I point first to the advocacy groups which I have previously mentioned and which also happen to be the two most powerful advocacy groups in the country—the NRA and AIPAC. While the vast majority of NRA members are responsible gun owners, and the NRA does encourage responsible gun practices, the most vocal wing of the organization consists of gun dealers who care only about being able to sell guns. So, the result is that the NRA takes a hard stand on being permitted to sell semiautomatic, magazine fed weapons, or equipment to convert rifles to lethal weapons, though most individual NRA members might actually agree that these weapons should be banned. I use the word "weapon" rather than "firearm" because we should make no mistake about it; these are weapons designed for mass killing of human beings. They are available because Congress is afraid of the NRA. It is interesting that the NRA has taken a stand against the 3D printing of unregistered firearm. These represent a threat to the sales of standard firearms.

AIPAC has Americans convinced that Israel is a noble ally of the United States, filled with good intentions but surrounded by evil enemies; but the Israeli government does not seem eager to make any friends in the neighborhood. Israel had a chance to make a real and lasting peace through reasonable compromise, but the right wing leadership in Israel, which maintains power with the blessing of the United States, in effect said "No, we want it all", all of Jerusalem and all of the ancient Holy Land, and the people who have lived on that land for hundreds of years must move. This is clearly a policy of preferring one ethnic group over another, something which should be abhorrent to all descent, thinking people in the twenty-first century—Americans, Israelis, and Arabs; Christians, Jews, and Muslims included.

The NRA and AIPAC are the two largest advocacy groups in America. In both, the vast majority of individual members are good people, who are advocating for a cause in which they sincerely believe. NRA members believe that the Second Amendment is central to what the United States is and owning firearms is a sacred right. AIPAC members believe that Israel should be allowed to live in peace and flourish as a great nation. But both the NRA and AIPAC are mega-groups with unchecked power. Neither has any built-in incentive to ask "What is right?" "What is just?" or "What is best for society?"

These two are not unique. The American Medical Association protects the interests of doctors first, those of the public second. This organization is likely to oppose such ideas as government single payer health insurance, because that system might be less lucrative for physicians. Yet, when the AMA takes a political stand, many people assume that stand to be in the interest of society, especially because the AMA tells them that it is, and doctors don't lie. And while the AMA may have a vested interest in opposing government single payer health insurance, the huge, wealthy American health insurance industry would be faced with complete destruction by such a system. We can be certain that large insurance companies will use all their resources to convince Americans that the current system is the best in the world. It may be for the wealthiest American, but for most we could do much better. Still most people seem to believe what they hear often enough.

The fact that America cannot train enough doctors to serve its needs, but poaches doctors from third world countries, is disturbing to me. Why? Why don't we allow more students into medical school? Is it because the AMA wants to keep doctors in short supply in order to be certain that the remuneration for doctors remains at a particular level?

Doctors complain that the cost of malpractice insurance is extreme, and it is. A very few very large court awarded settlements in malpractice suits drive up medical costs for all Americans. I am not saying that the loved ones of an unfortunate person who dies because of malpractice should not receive a large settlement— perhaps $10 million, but not $100 million. Why doesn't Congress put a generous, but reasonable, cap on law suits involving malpractice in order to drive the cost of malpractice insurance down for the benefit of the 99.9+ percent of Americans who will never have an issue with malpractice? Do you think the American Bar Association would want that? Congress apparently doesn't think so.

The pharmaceutical industry has similar power to that of the AMA and the American Bar Association but needs to be coy in its advertisements, because it is not given the automatic assumption of goodwill which is afforded to the AMA. The simple, frightening problem is that it is possible that enough money can convince a majority of Americans about anything. The overarching problem is that we are a society of competing interests. The common good is not a goal that generates much interest when up against any financially powerful advocacy group.

Not Global Warming; Environmental Protection

Today's global warming debate is ridiculous. Is global warming happening? Certainly, it is measureable in the melting of glaciers in places like Greenland. Is it human caused? Probably, even highly probably. But if we say that global warming is definitely caused by man, we open the door for naysayers. In complete truth, we cannot say with 100% certainty that global warming is completely human caused. The earth's climate is known to have varied noticeably, even in the last 1000 years. I personally believe that global warming is the most critical issue effected by the increased use of fossil fuels, but there are other issues and more convincing arguments that can be made to support reimagining energy production and consumption.

What is lost in the global warming argument are more essential facts. First, fossil fuels are finite. They will run out someday in the not too distant future. You and I won't be around then, but our children's children might be. So it makes sense to move away from fossil fuels now while we can make a smooth transition, rather than forcing our progenies to make an abrupt, possibly painful change in the future. Then when we consider the environment in which we live, pollution of the air and water is poisoning us right now. The world got a jarring glimpse of a frightening future in 1952 when London experienced ten days of "pea soup" fog which was blamed for the deaths of 2000 people in fog so thick that "people could not see their own hands held in front on them, and in the Royal Albert

Hall, concert audiences were unable to see the orchestra."[78] We used to think about this, but no one seems to want to say anything about it now. Sure, in the United States we have cleaned it up some, but LA still has smog, and pollution is still measured in the atmosphere of most major cities. We even have a rating system, "pollution index," in major cities and "pollution warnings," days in which elderly and vulnerable people are directed to stay inside. With or without global warming, we should be concerned with how we will leave the planet for future generations. Renewable energy is sensible and reasonable in the long-run. It also makes some pragmatic sense in the here and now. Such things as electric vehicles will be much cheaper to operate soon, therefore, in demand. The countries which gain the lead in manufacture of electric vehicles will gain a big economic advantage over others in the near future. Renewable energy and cleaner air is the future, better sooner than later; better with the US leading than struggling to catch up.

Perspective--Lucky to Be Born; Lucky to Be an American

Americans are the most fortunate of fortunate people. We represent about 5% of the world's population but command half of the world's wealth. We should remember that we are privileged not entitled. I feel that, as a result, I should be grateful and generous, not stingy and jealous.

More than this, the very existence of any one of us is an incredible miracle. That humans evolved and survived was only a small link in the succession of coincidences that led to you and me. After a couple million years and hundreds of generations, unique combinations of DNA came together to make you and me. Every individual alive today is a miracle of nearly infinite combinations. We should all celebrate our existence and be thrilled with having been given the opportunity to experience life. If we have had the additional benefit of good health, that should also be celebrated for as long as it lasts. I don't believe that there is an afterlife, but life on earth and all the luck which brought it about should be enough. Being an American and a boomer are bonuses.

---

[78] Phelps and Courtenay-Thompson, managing editors, p. 189.

This Boomer's Favorites

My favorite movies and books are those which I feel inspire the best of humanity and stimulate thought while providing excellent entertainment. I list these movies and books here for the inspiration they may provide you. I also list the websites which I have found can provide anyone anywhere with a first class education.

Favorite Movies

This list is ordered from first to tenth.

1. *Casablanca* with Humphrey Bogart and Ingrid Berman, 1942

    It's a little corny, but it's packed with symbolism. Ingrid Bergman looks like an angel, and the theme is admirable—in times of crisis, the individual sometimes has to put aside his own feelings and do what's right.

2. *The Americanization of Emily,* James Garner and Julie Andrews

    This film speaks honestly. It contains some interesting speeches, and it has humor and heart.

3. *The God's Must Be Crazy,* and *The Gods Must Be Crazy 2*

    This is clever and innovative. The main star is an African bushman who had only recently had contact with the outside world.

    Rarely is a sequel as good as the first movie, but this one is. The kids in it are adorable. But don't bother with the next two sequels. They stink.

4. *Raiders of the Lost Ark* with Harrison Ford and Karen Allen

    This is the perfect action-adventure movie.

5. *Indiana Jones and the Temple of Doom* with Harrison Ford and Kate Capshaw

    The opening song and dance number is beautifully

done and the action beginning is fast and fascinating. Kate Capshaw is beautiful throughout.

6. *The Great Dictator* with Charlie Chaplin, 1940
    This is a spoof on Adolf Hitler and the Nazis. The physical comedies is extremely well done. The names which Chaplin uses to parody leading Nazis are also clever.

7. *Star Trek IV: The Voyage Home* with William Shatner and Leonard Nimoy
    The crew of the Enterprise goes back to the late 20th century. The cultural dissonance provides opportunities for some great lines.

8. *Invictus* with Morgan Freeman and Matt Damon
    The story of noble efforts by Nelson Mandela to unite South Africa in support of a national rugby team and the achievements of that team with special attention to the thoughts and words of Mandela.

9. *Gettysburg* with Jeff Daniels
    This is an adaptation of the novel *Killer Angels,* an excellent account of the largest and most important battle every fought on US soil with emphasis on the greater meaning of the battle and the courage which may have saved the Union.

10. *Toy Story*
    This film is wonderfully innovative and the art work is nicely done.

Other Favorite Movies I Recommend Highly

The Adventures of Robin Hood with Errol Flynn
Great direction on the sword fighting scenes.

Doctor Strangelove with Peter Sellers
Wonderful spoof on the Cold War with Peter Sellers in two of the staring rolls.

Play it Again Sam with Woodie Allen and Diane Keaton
Charming comedy with therapeutic value.

Sleeper with Woodie Allen and Diane Keaton
Woodie Allen doing his best slapstick.

Annie Hall with Woodie Allen and Diane Keaton
Winner of four major Academy Awards. Thoughtful, intelligent, and funny.

Doctor Zhivago with Omar Sharif
From the epic novel about the Russian Revolution. Entertainment that educates.

Doctor No with Sean Connery
The first James Bond film with all the Bond gimmicks.

From Russia with Love with Sean Connery
The second James Bond film. Bond continued after this because this was as good as the first.

Blazing Saddles by Mel Brooks

This started a new trend in comedy—outrageousness that did not take itself seriously, but had a good heart.

Young Frankenstein by Mel Brooks
Mel Brooks' follow-up to *Blazing Saddles*. Some people say this this is even better.

Reds with Warren Beatty and Diane Keaton
Done as if it were in part a documentary, it is a true story John Reed, the only American buried in the Kremlin, his romantic partner, Louise Bryant, and the Russian Revolution. Long but extremely well done. Entertaining and educational.

Manhattan with Woodie Allen and Diane Keaton
Exceptional black-and-white photography and an incredible soundtrack are the key elements of this film.

Indiana Jones and the Last Crusade with Harrison Ford and Sean Connery
This isn't quite as good as the first two Indiana Jones movies, but it's still pretty good. I like it especially because the last scenes were filmed in Petra, Jordan, a "Wonder of the World" site which I have visited.

The Blues Brothers with John Belushi and Dan Aykroyd
A tribute to R&B music featuring James Brown, Ray Charles, Aretha Franklin, Cab Calloway, and others. The Blues Brothers Band staring Belushi and Aykroyd is also worth listening to of itself.

The Life of Brian by Monty Python
An intelligent, irreverent spoof on the New Testament, with a nearly plausible storyline.

Star Trek 2: The Wrath of Khan with William Shatner, Leonard Nimoy, and Ricardo Montalban
A good action movie and true to the original *Star Trek* formula.

Eraser with Arnold Schwarzenegger
My favorite Schwarzenegger movie.

The Big Chill with an ensemble cast of 1980s stars

150

The ensemble cast features several actors who went on to be big stars and some who almost did. The 60s Motown music is a big part of this movie about boomers, living lives that seem to lack something.

Bulworth with Warren Beatty and Holly Berry
This movie is little known, but well worth watching. It's about a Congressman, who is thrown into a part of society of which he knows nothing.

Saving Private Ryan with Tom Hanks
The Normandy invasion scenes at the beginning are very well done and moving.

Golden Eye with Pierce Brosnan
Die Another Day with Pierce Brosnan
For years no James Bond could compare to Sean Connery, but Pierce Brosnan managed the task and modern film making made these bond film the best of all.

Die Hard with Bruce Willis
My favorite Christmas movie. An excellent action drama.

Shanghai Noon with Jacky Chan and Owen Wilson
Rush Hour with Jacky Chan and Chris Tucker
Jackie Chan's two best films. Both are funny and both have these well-choreographed fight scenes.

Live Free or Die Hard with Bruce Willis
The best of all the *Die Hard* installments.

Avatar
An entertaining allegory about American aggression toward indigenous people.

Australia with Hugh Jackman and Nicole Kidman
An epic tribute to the country down under.

The Best Exotic Marigold Hotel
A rare film about older adults for adults, this has charm and class.

Captain America with Chris Evens
A fun fantasy with lots of action, humor, and a healthy dose of patriotism.

Inside-Out-animation
A cute and clever look into the mind of a pre-teen.

Coco-animation
Centered around events on the Day of the Dead, this is a lively tribute to Mexican traditions, and it has enough surprise and drama to be good entertainment.

Black Panther with Chadwick Boseman, Lupita Nyong'o, Michael B. Jordan
Given different circumstances, this is an alternative version of an African society. The characters are engaging, believable, and admirable.

Websites Anyone Can Use to Get a First Class Education Free

www.edx.org
www.coursera.org
www.futurelearn.com
www.khanacademy.com

Favorite Authors and Favorite Books

Dan Brown
Da Vinci Code; Inferno; Origin; Deception Point; Angels and Demons; The Lost Symbol (in that order)

Malcom Gladwell
David and Goliath; Tipping Point; Outliers; Blink (in that order)

Plato
Republic (If the "Allegory of the Cave" isn't the greatest story ever told, it's second. It encapsulates the root cause of all human folly.)

Jimmy Carter
Palestine: Peace Not Apartheid; Why Not the Best; We Can Have Peace in the Holy Land (in that order)

Robert Bellah
The Good Society; Habits of the Heart (in that order)

David Fromkin
A Peace to End All Peace
A thorough accounting of how the Versailles Peace settlement, ending World War I, set the stage for a century of violence.

John Meacham
The Soul of America: The Battle for Our Better Angels

Candice Millard
Destiny of the Republic: A Tale of Madness, Medicine and the Murder of a President

Ronald Takaki
Double Victory: A Multicultural History of America in World War II
(This is about the best of America; what America has been, could, and should be.)

Thomas Friedman
The World is Flat: A Brief History of the Twenty-first Century

Barbara Tuchman
The Guns of August

Adam Hochschild
To End All Wars: A Story of Loyalty and Rebellion, 1914-1918

Thomas E. Ricks
Churchill & Orwell: The Fight for Freedom

Michael Shaara
The Killer Angels: A Classic Novel of the Civil War

Photo Gallery: A Window to the World

  The two smaller buttons are for Eisenhower. They are normal size. The large buttons are both from the 1964 campaign. They encapsulate the main themes well. Lyndon Johnson emphasized that he would not be an extremist like Goldwater. As the election approached, polling showed Johnson with much greater support than Goldwater. Goldwater backers asserted that the polls were wrong, because many people who favored Goldwater were reluctant to state their support publically.

Jordan, 2005-2007

Breakfast with falafel, hummus, tomato, thyme, olives, olive oil, a sweet, eggs, French fries, and flat bread.

Our source of heat, propane. Our shower room and toilet room.

Doing the laundry. Baking a cake without an oven.

The living room, lounging on the farsha. The picture is that of King Hussein, the third king of Jordan who ruled for about 50 years and is considered to be "the father of his country."

With friends and neighbors.

Olive trees are abundant in northwest Jordan. Olive picking season is a major family project. Nearly every village has an olive factory where people take their olives to be pressed into olive oil.

Wedding parties are the focus of social life in the villages. But, as everything else in Jordan, most of the party is separate for men and women. Men dance the depka all night long.

The girls' school. Girls wear uniforms in school; boys do not. Girls who have not reached puberty often do not wear the head scarf. Nearly all Muslim women in the villages wear the head scarf though it is not formally required by law or by Islam.

I don't smoke, but peer pressure in Jordan got me smoking the tobacco hookah (water pipe) on this rare occasion. The sheep herding is part of farming in many villages.

Hadrian's gate at the Roman ruins in Jerash. The Roman Road through Jerash was lined with columns, many of which still stand today. What is more interesting is that these columns, which have been in place for nearly 2000 years, are free standing on their bases. I could wedge a spoon under the column as shown here, and see the spoon go up and down as the column swayed in the wind.

Petra, the pre-Roman city carved out of solid rock which is now considered to be a "wonder of the world." The climactic scenes of *Indiana Jones and the Last Crusade* were filmed here. The mysterious entrance to Petra is the "Siq", a one kilometer long crack in the mountains. This secret entrance protected the Nabatean people from the Romans for many years.

Our Egyptian Vacation

The pyramids at Giza.

The statues at Luxor.

Albania, 2013-2015

Village and the Shkumbin River. The heads are in memory of two Albanians killed by the now hated communist government. The tadpoles hatch on the river in April.

The mountain town of Berat.

Performers in traditional costume.

Skanderbeg statue in Skanderbeg Square, the center of the Albanian capital, Tirana. Skanderbeg is the national hero of Albania.

The Albanian Communist dictator, Enver Hoxha, had a pyramid built in Tirana to honor himself. It's a concrete monster and the current government has struggled with what to do with it. In the meantime it has become a fun challenge for thrill seekers climbing to the top. That is me at the top, but I didn't do the graffiti.

George W. Bush Street (upper left)

Albanians love America.The building is the Abraham Lincoln Development Center. The statue is Woodrow Wilson, who supported Albanian independece at the Versaille Peace Conference of 1919.

Albanian national hero, Skanderbeg, outside the Skanderbeg Museum in Kruja where Skanderbeg had his castle, the headquarters of the Albanian resistance to the Ottoman Empire.

The statue of Ismail Qemali in Valore. Qemali is the political leader who decared indedendence from the Ottoman Empire in Valore in 1913.

Remnants of the Cold War. "Social Realism" statues can be found in Tirana covered and hidden. A half million bunkers dot the countryside throughout Albanian. One has even been moved to the center of Tirana for exhibit and as a tribute to the fall of communism, as has been a slab of the Berlin Wall.

Cinnabun was the only American franchise restaurant in Albania when I was there, but there were lots of look alikes and imposters in Tirana—McDonalds, Hard Rock Café, AFC, Subway, Cheers, McDonalds look alike.

A nice bar and restaurant near the University of Tirana and the American Embassy. Notice the Albanian flag on the right.

City wall and Albanian flag in Elbasan, Albania and the University of Berat.

The power grid in Tirana.

Saint Theresa at Mother Theresa Square in Tirana. The Albanian nun who ministered to the poor in India.

Vietnam, 2016-2017

Ho Chi Minh City (formerly Saigon).The photo of Ho is in the central post office.

Celebrations. Christmas at the Saigon Mall. Tet, the Vietnamese New Year. High School prom at our American school.

The beach at Da Nang. The sign advertises the Asian Pacific Leaders Conference, which was attended by important world leaders, including the President of the United States.

The swastika was an ancient symbol used by Buddhism, Hinduism, and Jainism before it was appropriated by Nazi Germany.

The Catholic Cathedral of Hanoi at Christmas 2017.

Ha Long Bay World Heritage site.

Angkor Wat Buddhist temple complex World Heritage Site in Cambodia.

Mysterious entrances to Angkor Wat temples.